P9-DWZ-370

E
A
R
T
H

World at War A
L
I
E
N
S

S.E. Wendel

EPIC
Press

World at War
Earth Aliens: Book #5

Written by S.E. Wendel

Copyright © 2016 by Abdo Consulting Group, Inc.

Published by EPIC Press™
PO Box 398166
Minneapolis, MN 55439

Cover design by Dorothy Toth
Images for cover art obtained from iStockPhoto.com
Edited by Clete Barrett Smith

LIBRARY OF CONGRESS CATALOGING-IN-PUBLICATION DATA

Wendel, S.E.
World at war / S.E. Wendel.
p. cm. — (Earth aliens ; #5)
Summary: Everything's changed now that more humans have come, and they bring
the devastating news that Earth's atmosphere was destroyed by a solar flare. If all
goes according to plan, the humans will finally take their place as dominant species
of Terra Nova.
ISBN 978-1-68076-026-2 (hardcover)
1. Aliens—Fiction. 2. Human-alien encounters—Fiction.
3. Extraterrestrial beings—Fiction. 4. Science fiction.
5. Young adult fiction. I. Title.
[Fic]—dc23
2015903969

To my mother, who I can never thank enough for typing a seven-year-old's dictations

The afternoon was clear and quiet. Looking down upon Karak, her mountain-city, the leader of the Charneki, the young *mara*, stood upon one of the great palace balconies overlooking the whole southern face of the city. Zeneba sighed, and her chest felt constricted. She could feel every rib.

She rubbed her bleary eyes, trying to brush off her tiredness. Four days ago it had happened again. Beings, demons from the sky, rained down upon their land. The Charneki had been at war with the first group of demons for over a cycle now—more could only mean trouble. It was all she could do not to sink down and cry.

As *mara,* all looked to her for guidance and strength. It had been predicted, when she was just a *maheen,* newly arrived in Karak, that she would see the end of an age. She stood on that abyss now, and it was dark and desolate.

"Golden One."

Turning at the sound of Yaro's voice, she nodded at the Head of her Guard. A quiet warrior, Yaro was her most loyal friend these past years and had become invaluable to her in this time of trial. He had spent time in demon captivity, taken during a sabotage mission in the north. She still felt grateful every time she saw him to have him back.

Standing beside Yaro was an interesting little creature. Small, pinky, with a mop of brown hair atop his head, he was an otherworldly thing. A demon himself, Rhys was a precocious young human who proved a valuable prisoner. He and a small group of demons had brought Yaro back to Karak some time ago, and she had kept most of them, threatening that for every Charneki killed she would execute one human. That had been a dark time.

Rhys bowed to her. "Hello, *mara.*"

"Good day to you, Rhys."

She had been itching to speak with him for days now, but her people came first. Though it had been their second experience with falling stars, the Charneki were still very new to the idea of other beings existing past the sky. Mass hysteria had gripped Karak, and Zeneba spent most of her time consoling, explaining, and soothing. She received delegations from all of the closest clans, assuring them that scouts would be sent and the capital would stand firm.

"You look tired, *mara.*"

Yaro grunted at the little human's familiarity.

Zeneba grinned wryly. "There has been little time for sleep, little *plarra.*"

"I understand," he said in his odd accent.

Rhys had learned the Charneki language from the queen's own brother, Zaynab. The two became friends when she travelled north to retake the tundra region. Zaynab had been slain just before the Charneki were pushed back south, something she couldn't forgive herself for, not even now. It was amazing, though, to learn that this little demon had been so touched by Zaynab and grieved alongside her at his death.

"I want you to explain what is happening," she said. "I want to understand."

He shifted his weight from one foot to the other and glanced down at the ground before speaking. "More humans have come, *mara*."

"From your old home?"

"Yes."

"Why have they come? Did you send for them?"

"It was the idea, *mara*, for many to come."

She frowned, not understanding.

He thought a moment then pushed his sleeve up to reveal what the demons called gauntlets. They weren't like any gauntlet the Charneki could make. A metal contraption, the gauntlet stored all of the human's knowledge, which could be called forth in a matter of moments by requesting the information. Zeneba still didn't quite understand the device; the idea of it made her head hurt sometimes.

Pressing his fingers to the gauntlet surface in a pattern of movements, he created a floating picture. Zeneba held in her gasp at the sudden appearance, still startled though she had seen this done before. Yaro looked on warily, the muscles in his long neck tensing.

"This is *Earth*—our old home."

Zeneba marveled at the floating picture. It was a dust-colored orb surrounded by a blanket of stars set in black.

"Where do you live?" she asked.

"Humans live on top," he said, pointing at the whole surface. "It is a big *planet*."

"*Planet*," she said, repeating the human word. It felt odd on her tongue.

He nodded. "Earth is a planet. A big circle of ground and water. Charnek is a planet too."

She told him to explain himself.

After another combination of finger taps, a new floating picture sprung at her. It was similar to the other, but this orb was green and blue. She marveled at the image and slowly came to realize she recognized the northern landmass. She had seen it on Charneki maps.

"I don't . . . " She waved her hands in front of her face in confusion.

"It is much," Rhys said. "But that is the truth. Charnek is a planet humans could live on top of too."

What this all meant Zeneba couldn't fathom. She had rationalized that the humans' old home, this Earth, existed further than the sky. First there were the clouds, then Nahara and Undin, the Charneki's beloved sun deities, in their Sunned Realm with a royal host of glittering attendant stars. But after? It was too much.

"Earth used to look like Charnek," Rhys was saying, bringing up yet another floating picture.

This time it was a second blue and green sphere. It seemed a perfect cross between the first two images—same landmasses and forms as the first but the coloring of the second.

"This was Earth five hundred cycles ago."

Zeneba's eyes went wide as Rhys returned to the first picture.

"This is Earth now."

Her mouth hung open. Such a difference!

"What happened?" she asked in horror.

"It is dead," Rhys said quickly. He sniffed.

She looked down upon him, shocked by his words. His bluntness didn't hide the pain behind his eyes.

For a moment she couldn't speak, though her mouth moved as if to form words. Finally she forced out, "How?"

He glanced up at her, his cheeks burning red and his eyes glassy. "We killed it."

An infectious excitement gripped the expedition when they saw the gleaming starships spearing the clear blue sky. Hugh O'Callahan's pulse thrummed in his ears as he followed the caravan, guiding the speeder he drove towards the seven pinnacles of human technology.

The gunner sitting behind him, his friend Elena Ames, slapped his shoulder. For once he didn't argue about speeding up.

The expedition came from the southern jungles, having made the month-long journey in an attempt to forge an alliance with the Tikshi people. They had quickly learned humans weren't the only intelligent species on Terra Nova; two native species existed, the Charneki, whom the humans had been at war with almost from the outset, and the Tikshi who, if they were to be believed, had been warring with the Charneki since the beginning of creation. An alliance was agreed upon, but the expedition had cut festivities short—much to the chagrin of the Tikshi, who had been amid their ten-day celebration—when they saw seven starships break atmo.

As they neared the starships, Hugh saw their landing had been much cleaner than the first colony's, all the starships landing within a few square miles of each other. The huge bay doors were open, and people milled about in groups, marveling at the green world. A tent city had already been erected.

A command flashed onto the screen embedded in the dash, just in front of his seat. Glancing down, Hugh read that they were to follow Colonel Klein, head of the expedition and second-in-command of the first colony's military regime, in his lead cruiser to the western side.

Approaching from the southeast, the caravan adjusted course, skirting the perimeter. They caught the gaze of several people walking about. When the new colonists saw them they raised their hands and smiled.

Veering in close to one of the starships, Hugh saw they were headed for another group of vehicles.

As they came into sight, a formidable woman jumped from the passenger seat of a cruiser and stood waiting for them.

Hugh wasn't surprised to see General Hammond there, but it did dampen his spirits slightly to see her. She had been the leader of their seven-year journey to Terra Nova and seized control of the colony, New Haven, after they arrived when she refused to hold democratic elections.

Easing the speeder to a stop, Hugh killed the engine and waited for directions. He could feel Elena's intense desire to hop down and start walking about; it radiated from her, and he felt the small vibrations her tapping fingers made on the mounted gun.

Colonel Klein slid out of his cruiser and greeted General Hammond. They shared smiles and a few quiet words before the colonel turned back to the expedition.

"Take a break, but don't get lost."

That was all the expedition needed, and everyone was from the vehicles in a moment.

Waiting the half second it took Elena to hop down off the backseat, the two of them followed the others along the outskirts of the new colony.

Hugh stared up in awe at the nearest starship. It had been a while since he had seen a starship—their four had been broken down to build, supply, and run New Haven. Everything about the starships had been planned with repurposing in mind. These new starships seemed even bigger than the originals, and as Hugh looked about, he swore there were significantly more colonists. Of course there were seven ships this time, but if they were in fact bigger, they most likely brought more humans.

He and Elena shared a look between them, grinning. There was something relieving about seeing the new colony. They weren't alone anymore.

"How long do you think it'll take her?" Elena asked quietly, nodding at the general.

"Not long."

He refused to be too worried about the general right now—everyone could guess she was already thinking about how to make these new arrivals work for her in the war against the Charneki. From what Hugh understood, they hadn't been able to communicate with the second expedition, so these first few days of contact would be crucial for the general and her agenda.

Strolling along the grassy edge of a starship crater, Hugh and Elena came across a group of three people, two women and a man. They smiled as Hugh and Elena approached.

"Hi there!"

"Hello," Hugh said.

Elena nodded, trying her best at a smile. Elena never found small talk easy.

"You're from the other colony, right?" asked one of the women.

"Yup. New Haven."

They smiled at the name. "Now that's apropos," the man said.

"How're you feeling?" Hugh asked.

"It's good to be off," the second woman said. "It was a long trip."

"Were you awake?" asked Elena.

The first woman and man nodded.

"So were we," Hugh said.

The man looked between the two of them, surprised. "You must've been kids when you left Earth."

"Yeah, something like that."

"How do you like it here?" asked the second woman. "We're all so excited—it's better than we could've imagined!"

"It's something else," Hugh said, exchanging a glance with Elena. They both weren't sure if they should mention the tangled political situation the new arrivals unwittingly inherited with their new home.

"How far away is New Haven?"

"About thirty miles northwest," Elena said, pointing in the general direction.

"Has it been hard?" asked the man. "Adjusting, I mean."

Hugh shook his head. "We managed. Terra Nova is what we hoped for as far as being a new Earth. But it's different, certainly."

"Are there more coming?" Elena asked.

The mood palpably shifted, the three of them paling. They looked at one another, their mouths opening then closing, as if words escaped them.

Finally the man, unable to look at Hugh or Elena, cleared his throat and said, "About a year out we got a transmission. Earth's atmosphere gave out."

Hugh and Elena stood there in stunned silence. He supposed he should have anticipated this—the breakdown of Earth's atmosphere was the reason he, his brother Rhys, Elena, all of them left in the first place. When the first wave departed, it was predicted a livable atmosphere would last maybe a decade more. If he thought it through, the scientists had been pretty close—sometimes he forgot how long he had been gone.

Elena recovered first. "So that's it then."

"Most likely. We think some people still survive indoors, since the transmission had to be sent by somebody. But nothing's sustainable anymore."

Hugh stood with Elena and the three new arrivals in a deafening silence, wondering how it came to this. He looked up at the sky, and though the bright blue afternoon hid the stars, he imagined he could see that third planet from the sun.

His heart panged. For the first time in quite a while, Hugh found himself thinking about his mother. Her face was that of a ghost, something from another life. When he looked up, he thought about the immeasurable distance between him and whatever remained of her, and his chest felt hollow, as if ribs surrounded a cavity of nothing.

The desire to see his brother overwhelmed him. They had boarded their starship as twin eleven-year-olds, but while Hugh had been assigned to an apprenticeship under the head engineer, Mikhail Saranov, Rhys was put to cryogenic sleep. When they arrived on Terra Nova, Hugh was almost nineteen, Rhys still eleven. It was a gap between them that never closed.

Now Rhys was miles away, a prisoner in the Charneki capital. At least he hoped. Elena had been one of the few to return from that failed diplomatic mission, bearing the Charneki queen's threat. The expedition had killed more than enough Charneki during their journey south for the queen to have executed all her human captives.

All this wasn't important anymore. Hugh didn't care about politics or sides, morals or justice. Rhys, if it hadn't been true before, was now all he had left of Earth, of their mother, and he wanted him back.

2

Hopping down off the gunner's seat of the speeder, Elena Ames stretched out her back, waiting for the satisfying *pop* before looking about.

They had spent two days with the new colony, helping out wherever they were needed. General Hammond insisted upon putting up a perimeter, but the new colony's expedition leader, Tanaka Kimura, decided other things came first.

It was interesting to learn that Kimura wasn't military, but civilian. One of the top engineers from Dawning Enterprises, the corporation that had funded, built, and supplied the two expeditions, he was technically a company official rather than a military hire-on. Word was that Kimura had been instrumental in the design of the second round of starships, fixing what could have been a "potentially catastrophic engine failure." Those of New Haven already knew plenty about that. One of their starships had erupted mid-flight, taking with her over nine-thousand people.

Finally home in New Haven, Elena felt a sort of relief. They had been gone for over two months now, and it hadn't been an easy absence. The Terra Novan landscape was untamed and foreign, presenting challenges every opportunity it got. Not to mention the Charneki hadn't exactly let them pass through unscathed—two ambushes left over a dozen humans and more than a hundred Charneki dead.

"Should we head to sick bay?" Elena asked Hugh.

Though Hugh had already been seen by several doctors, their own on the expedition and two in the new colony's makeshift medical tent, Elena still worried over the wound he got from a Charneki arrow. It almost went right through his upper chest, just below his left collarbone. Despite sustaining heavy casualties during the march south, Colonel Klein hadn't allowed them to turn back.

Hugh nodded. "I think that'd be good. It's feeling prickly."

They were about to move off when Klein's voice stopped them. "That'll have to wait. Everyone's going to an official address."

It was an order, not a suggestion. Elena and Hugh exchanged looks before falling in line with the others of the expedition. She looked about and saw tired faces and drooping eyes. It had been an exhausting mission, and there were others like Hugh who really should be getting to sick bay.

Leaving the hangar, the group was one of several headed from the military quadrant out east, just beyond the residential quadrant, to a levelled, open field they created during construction.

Native grasses poked through the cold dirt, feeling the advent of spring. Usually the field was used as a sort of park, with people walking about or eating lunch. Sometimes the field held games and tournaments, spectators sitting on the grassy berm, once the slope of a starship crater, overlooking the field, and once in a while General Hammond used it as a platform for her rare public, mandatory addresses, as it was the only place in New Haven large enough to fit forty thousand colonists.

"You were right," Elena whispered, "not long at all."

The field was already full, and they joined the other military personnel grouping towards the front on the west side. The general always liked her loyalists close to her, just in case things went south. And they usually did.

There was an excited buzz in the crowd. For once this would be good news, and everyone seemed anxious to hear about the new colony.

General Hammond didn't keep them waiting

much longer, mounting a temporary platform. As she came to stand in the center, gazing out onto the crowd, a large projection of her upper half splayed out on either side of her.

She wasn't a very tall woman, but the raised platform worked to her benefit. She always had her fair hair pulled back in a tight bun, accenting the sharp angles of her face and cold glint of her gray eyes.

"Good morning," she said, her voice booming across the field from a hidden mic and speakers. "I have wonderful news for you today. As you have heard, another wave of colonists arrived safely on Terra Nova nineteen days ago. They landed thirty-three miles southeast of us and are in the beginning stages of construction. There are seven starships in total, and one hundred twenty-five thousand colonists. A registry of both their colony and ours will be made available shortly, and I encourage everyone to check these to see if any names are familiar. There is a great deal for them to do, and we will help wherever we can."

A round of applause went through the crowd, and Elena considered it a historic moment.

In her normal fashion, however, the general lost everything she just gained.

"This new colony is vulnerable. As the vanguard, it's our duty to ensure that they are protected against the native threat."

The crowd went silent, but General Hammond pressed on.

"They are new to this world, and I will be working closely with their expedition leader to make sure they understand the gravity of the native threat. I understand how many of you feel about my policies, especially concerning the natives, and I hope now to convince you. While this is a time of celebration—indeed, it's further proof of human ingenuity and superiority—it comes with a double edge. I must tell you now that Earth is no more."

The general paused, letting the news sink in. If

there had been any small noises before, they were dead in an instant. Elena considered those closest to her, saw shocked, pale faces.

"I've confirmed it with Tanaka Kimura, and it's as we feared. Six Earth years ago, a solar storm destroyed several layers of atmosphere. The Earth we knew is dead. For now we grieve—all we know is gone. But there is still hope. *We* have lived. *We* carry with us everything that was beautiful about Earth and all those who died there. They live on in us. And they are precious. They need to be protected. This is our last chance at survival—we must do things right this time and ensure the success of generations to come. You're here because someone else isn't. Don't dishonor that sacrifice. I'm not asking you to kill natives. I'm asking you to help safeguard the human race's survival.

"I know this is a lot to take in, and I understand what you must be feeling. Earth was our home. But Terra Nova is our salvation. All I ask is that you fight to defend our chance. It's our last one.

I know I won't have convinced some of you—I know what you think of me. But I will ask those who want to see the success of this colony volunteer their services. We will be holding sign-ups for open military personnel positions, and I hope to see many of you. Please, the future is in our hands. Thank you, and good day."

She left a sort of stunned silence in her wake, and Elena was surprised to see a shift in the crowd. For once things hadn't devolved into a shouting match between the general and Ulysses Carter, the unofficial leader of a growing opposition movement. General Hammond's words, Elena had to admit, were inspiring. She chose well, had done it perfectly. Elena would be interested to see how many new recruits the regime got out of this.

"Well that was . . . "

Hugh nodded, agreeing with what she didn't have to say. "It's still hard to believe," he said quietly.

"I guess we just thought it wouldn't actually happen."

They stood together as the crowd began to disperse, heading back to homes and jobs.

Elena raised her head when she heard her name called. Looking around, she finally spotted a little hand waving excitedly deep in the crowd.

Skipping towards them was Cassandra Tran. She, Elena, and Hugh had been close friends since their time aboard ship, all serving apprenticeships together. Cass had recently come into her own as a budding scientist, taking over the management of many key projects from her former mentor and boss, Dr. Oswald, who was one of those held captive in the Charneki capital.

Cass leapt at Elena, wrapping her arms around her neck and giggling. She released her after a moment, knowing Elena's rule about physical contact duration, and went on to Hugh. When she was finally done with the bear hugs, she beamed up at them.

"How the hell are you?" she said, her eyes glittering.

Her intense enthusiasm was so starkly different from the attitude of others around them that Elena felt overwhelmed by it.

"Glad to be back," Elena said.

Cass's eyes widened. "How're you?" she asked Hugh, indicating his wound. "Shouldn't you be at sick bay?"

"That's my next stop, I promise."

She gave him a comically overdone scowl. "Good. Just what I wanted to hear. You'd better not die on me."

"It's not on my agenda."

"How're things here?" Elena asked.

Cass shrugged. "For the most part, same old. But of course we've had our hands full the past few days. It's pretty amazing that they were able to get a second expedition off the ground so quick."

Hugh cleared his throat. "Cass, have you . . . " He lowered his voice, "Have you heard anything about Rhys?"

Cass's face went from day to night. Her gaze dropped.

"Oh god, what's—?"

"We haven't heard anything official," Cass said quickly before he could jump to conclusions.

"What's that mean?"

She swallowed. "We lost communication with Dr. Oswald about two weeks ago. Apparently he had been talking with General Hammond for some time."

In everything that had already gone on with that abysmal diplomatic mission, Elena didn't know why this shouldn't be added to the heap. Elena hadn't been entirely sure why she was chosen for the mission, and her commanding officer, Sgt. Rhiannon White, had been suspicious of those assigned to go, citing that they were chosen from everywhere without much rhyme or reason. Then she had pieced together from Hugh's dehydrated babbling, for he had come after them on his own and nearly killed himself, that most of those chosen to go were considered undesirable by the regime, many harboring softer feelings about the Charneki. It explained why Rhys, a thirteen-year-old, would be allowed to go, with or without his linguistic ability.

"And she did nothing?" Hugh demanded.

Cass looked around before replying, "I think she thought he was more valuable there."

"Was?" Elena repeated.

Cass glanced at her, and she saw she was fighting tears.

"W-we suspect he's been killed."

Hugh's mouth fell open, and he took a step back. He put his hands on his head and groaned unintelligible syllables.

Seeing what she had done, Cass quickly put a hand on Hugh's shoulder and said, "Th-that doesn't mean anyone else's been hurt. Hugh, we just don't know anything."

Elena put her own hand on Hugh's other shoulder and filled her fist with his jacket. She pulled on him until he looked at her. Terrified that he would fall back into the depression that had kept him in his apartment for two weeks after learning of Rhys's capture, Elena knew she had to say something, anything to make this better.

"Don't assume," she said. "It's like Cass says, we don't know anything for sure."

"But you said yourself—the queen would kill one for every native we killed." His face contorted. "We killed so many . . . "

"Hey," she said, pushing him again. "If anyone is going to survive, it's Rhys. He knows the natives."

"Speaking the language doesn't—"

"You and I both know it's more than that. He understands them. Maybe Oswald was caught or something. We don't know. But Hugh, I know this—the queen wouldn't kill Rhys. He's different."

And she hoped to god that stayed true.

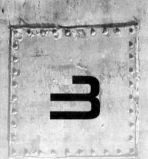

3

The procession of the clans was something to behold, banners of all sizes and colors flapping in the morning breeze. Zeneba stood on the top tier of the palace, waiting for them on the landing of the great staircase that started as Karak's main promenade all the way down in the harbor and led straight up to the palace.

Her heart swelled to see so many had answered her call. It surely hadn't been an easy journey for some, and what they had come to hear wouldn't cheer them.

All manner of trumpets and horns sounded the arrival of the first clans in the harbor, and the mountain-horns answered in a bellow. The sound was a rich, comforting one. It was the sound of the ancestors, of all those who had come before.

"It's a good sign," she said to Yaro, "don't you think?"

"They are anxious to see their *mara*."

"And I them."

The rhythmic march made her heart beat loudly in her a chest, and her skin shimmered a deep purple, the happiest hue she had worn in quite some time. Perhaps the most alluring thing about the tall Charneki was their swirls of iridescent skin. The pattern was different for each individual and could go through a number of colors depending upon emotion, though by the time of adulthood, the swirls settled into one color, reflecting personality, only to change with shifting feeling. Zeneba had been trained by the Elders, however, to control the *harn-da*, this skin-changing.

As the Brave Ones approached the palace, marching seven abreast in a column, the populace of Karak threw grains and grasses into the street, joyous at the sight of so many warriors. These were just the chieftains and their retinue, but so many had answered her call that the main promenade seemed full of Brave Ones.

When Zeneba looked out, she saw flashes of gold everywhere, a reflection of the happiness and assurance her people felt. It warmed her heart and firmed her resolve.

The first of the clans walked through the great jade gate of the palace, their hue a proud maroon. When all stood in position, gazing up at her, as one they raised their spears and banners and brought down the shafts, making a ring that shook the mountain itself. They raised two cries, placed their three-fingered fists over their hearts, and bowed their heads to her.

"Brave Ones," she said, her hands extended towards them, "it is not an auspicious occasion for your coming, but your presence brings us all hope.

I invite your chieftains to come with me into the Red Hall, and I will hear you."

"Bless your name, Zeneba Mara, the Gold-Hearted!" they cried.

Passing into the cool interior of the Red Hall, the topmost point of Karak, Zeneba walked through the turquoise-robed Elders already gathered there, making her way to her red seat. Carved from the top stone of Karak, it was a great piece of smoothed stone where all the *mari* and *maraii* had sat before her, all the way back to Yalah Mar, the Gold-Fist.

Sitting on a finely carved wooden chair beside her throne was the head of her council, her former tutor, the Skywatcher, Elder Zhora. His sightless, milky eyes followed the small noise of her feet as she passed through the Hall, finally coming to her throne.

As she sat, all present bowed low to her.

"It heartens me to see you all," she began. "I have called you here to represent your clans, to speak for all my people, and tell me what is said through the Marland. I want to know the thoughts and will of my people."

A broad Charneki with many battle scars stepped forward. His cuirass was the yellow of a *hunala* plant. He bowed to her. "Bless your name, Zeneba Mara," he said. "It is we who are heartened at the sight of our *mara*. We of the Juntana Plains are honored to answer your call."

"You are welcome here, Chieftain Baravar. Please, what news of the grasslands?"

"We have resisted the demons' push south, trying to contain them to their small farming outpost. This has seen success thus far, but the coming of more demons threatens to overwhelm us. I lost an entire garrison, *mara*, to the Tikshi and demons."

"It was a valiant effort, Chieftain, and I know your warriors rest with Nahara and Undin."

"Please, *mara*, has word come from the southern coasts yet? Has the alliance been struck?"

"It has, yes."

Uneasy mutterings buzzed in her ears.

"To speak on this, Chieftain Samuka, please step forward."

A young warrior in a burgundy cuirass answered her call. He had until recently been one of the captains of her Guard, but upon the death of Chieftain Loppa without a named successor, she had sent him to fill the position. She had first wanted to give it to Ondra, her childhood friend, but he refused it, wanting to stay in Karak with her.

Bowing, Chieftain Samuka said, "We believe their alliance was made several days before the demons returned north."

"They were able to cross your shores *twice*? Both times without your noticing?" demanded another chieftain, stepping forward.

She was an imposing figure, her cuirass a gleaming black and her eyes an uncommonly deep blue. All hushed at Chieftain Heta's words, and they stunned Zeneba.

"Leave the boy alone, Heta," said Chieftain Baravar. "He hasn't worn his gauntlets half as long as you or I. Besides, if *you* had stopped them in your rocky canyons, they might not have been his problem."

"Don't speak to me about such things, Baravar. You failed to stop them too," Chieftain Heta spat, her upper lip twitching.

Nodding at Yaro, who stood to Zeneba's right in his ceremonial position as her Head, he brought his heavy metal spear down, making the hall ring. This caused a sudden hush, which Zeneba was quick to take advantage of.

"Please, Chieftains, you speak angry words, but your grief runs deep. It is a shared grief. You have lost too many already. But I have not called you to lay blame on anyone."

Her jaw taut, Chieftain Heta bowed. "Forgive me, Golden One."

"There is nothing to forgive. But please, let us

continue. I am anxious to hear what you all have to say."

With several sharp words, Chieftain Heta related that the Charneki of Kol's Mouth, a vast stretch of rocky desert south of the Juntana Plains, were ready to fight the demons.

Many chieftains stepped forward, from the western coastal bluffs, to the eastern beaches, even Chieftain Numal, the leader of Zeneba's home in the eastern mountains, all professed their loyalty and willingness to see battle.

"Would my people have anything of me?" she asked.

Chieftain Numal, whom Zeneba had admired since she was a young *maheen*, said, "Please, *mara*, they want to understand what these new stars mean. Why have they come?"

She cleared her throat. "The demons need a new home. They had to leave their land and come a long way here in their stars."

"But why? Why did they have to leave?"

"Their land died. There was nothing they could do. To survive, they left."

"How do you know this, *mara*?" asked Chieftain Baravar.

Her mouth opened, but nothing came out at first. She wasn't entirely sure how they would react to this next part, and she worried about having to defend her decisions. She was actually rather intimidated by the steely eyes of Chieftain Heta.

"I have spoken with several demons. One young one in particular. He learned our language, and he told me of his dying land."

"It's true then," said Chieftain Heta, those fierce eyes narrowing. "You keep demons in Karak."

"For now," Zeneba said. "They came to me in peace. These seem different than the others. I hope that with them, we might forge a peaceful future. But this will come after we reclaim our land."

"How do you know they don't speak lies?" Chieftain Heta asked.

"He has no reason to lie."

"They could be spies!"

"One was, yes. But he was dealt with, and the others know the price of betrayal."

"But *why*? What makes this young demon worthy of your trust?"

Zeneba sat in silence, for she knew the answer would be too painful to utter. How could she tell her chieftains, all her Brave Ones, that she trusted Rhys because she trusted her brother?

"Your *mara* will do what she believes best for her people," said Yaro in a low growl. "You will trust her, Heta."

Yaro and Chieftain Heta glared at one another for a long moment, and finally Zeneba felt safe enough to continue.

"I wish you to ride back to your homes and people and tell them that their *mara* thinks of them and will deliver them from this time of uncertainty. The time has come to fight."

A great cry was raised at this, and many fists flew into the air.

"The danger is great, our enemy is powerful, but no cause is worthier than ours. We fight for our home, for our place in this world, and for that I ask you to ride into battle with me. Ride the wind, with Nahara at your backs, and raise me an army."

———————

Hoisting himself up onto the window ledge, Rhys O'Callahan balanced on the very tip of the toe of his boots. The city was electrified; he could feel it in the very stones of the mountain.

He wished he could be out there. Whatever the occasion was, it looked better than being cooped up in their converted storeroom. The human delegation had been kept in several places in Karak, namely dungeons and cells, and while their current room was certainly still a makeshift cell, it was a vast improvement regardless. However, the space was getting increasingly small for seventeen people; he suspected one more bitten nail or cracked knuckle would set off a chain reaction.

For a short time, they had had more freedom, but that ended when Rhys caught Dr. Oswald, the former head of the delegation, betraying crucial information to General Hammond. Rhys's throat caught whenever he thought about it; Dr. Oswald had tried to strangle him, and for this, the queen had him executed.

It was somewhat for their own safety, then, that they were confined. He knew they lost considerable ground with Dr. Oswald's death, and the queen admitted many wanted the lives of all the humans. He felt in his heart they had the queen's confidence, but for now, it was best to lie low.

"What's going on out there?" asked Cara, one of the scientists.

"I can't tell really—it's not a great view."

That was the truth. Their small windows overlooked a sheer cliff face. There were many other such windows lining the mountain all the way down to the waterline. That was part of the joy of living in a mountain—so many ways to fall off.

Pulling himself further up, Rhys shimmied until he got his head around the corner of the window. "It looks like a party," Rhys said.

"It might be some sort of festival," said Georgiana, the resident anthropologist. "It should be around the start of spring."

The sound of the lock grating out of place made them all look towards the door. Rhys just slid all of himself back into the room when the door opened.

Yaro walked through, quickly standing aside. The queen followed him in.

Rhys and the others bowed to her.

"*Yan amar, mara*," Rhys said. "Greetings."

"Hello, little *plarra*. How are you this day?"

"We are well, *mara*, thank you. You honor us with your presence."

"I believe you wanted to see me?"

In truth he was a little surprised to see her, what with the apparent celebration going on. He had managed to coax the guard to get Yaro to tell the queen that the humans had a proposition for her, but he hadn't expected her to come within the day.

Rhys grinned. "We have something to interest you."

"And what is that?"

"Please."

He motioned for her to come closer to one of the work tables that had been set up for their use. They had originally been working on medicine for the Charneki, Cara herself had discovered an antiviral for the native version of the flu. Now, with that project firmly on the back burner, Rhys agreed with the others that, while the queen might not think badly of them, something else would have to be offered up to get her more on their side.

"We have ideas for you."

"About what?" she asked, grinning at him.

Rhys arranged the blueprints—which amounted really to glorified sketches, given what they had to work with—before her.

"We call these *generators*."

She repeated the human word then asked, "What do they do?"

"They can do many things, *mara*. For us it is an old idea—humans have used them for many years. The ones in New Haven are very big and new, but we could build for you here a little one."

She traced one long finger over the drawings, her hairless brows slightly drawn together. Her purple swirls of skin didn't change to another color, but he saw its shifting brightness and hoped that was a good sign.

He glanced over his shoulder and grinned impishly at Yaro. The warrior nodded at him, but gave him a stern look, no doubt reminding him to behave himself.

"And what would I do with a *generator*?"

"Well, we . . . " He looked around, waved his hand quickly at two others. He introduced Perry, another scientist who had a knack for tinkering, and Katja, a military technician, to the queen. "We could use them for many things."

Telling Perry and Katja what he had just said, they stared at him and then the queen, rather starstruck. Katja recovered first, saying, "Well there's a lot they could do. It's a rudimentary way to make electricity, so first we could power lights."

"They say they could make light," Rhys translated for the queen. Recalling her initial negative reaction towards this proposition, the Charneki considering it offensive to their sun deities, Rhys added, "Dark does not have to be an uncertain time. We can make light to brighten the night if you wish. They could also light the inside of your mountain."

The queen leaned back, considering. "How much light could you make?"

Rhys smiled. "As much as you wish, *mara*.

He felt relieved to see no reaction like the original; instead he watched as she continued to let her eyes wander over the proposal. The seconds ticked by, and he hoped he had explained it well enough.

In truth, he was hopeless at understanding how a generator worked—that was Hugh's job, not his—or even knowing about all they could do, so taken for granted were they now.

Finally the queen nodded, and a grin spread across her face. "It is a good idea, little *plarra*. In fact, I may have something that will aid you. But first I must consult my Elders."

"Of course, *mara*," he said, bowing his head. His curiosity piqued at what the queen could have for them, but he chose to ask later, once the plan was underway.

"I will tell them of your idea in the morning."

"Thank you, *mara*." Rhys waved his hand behind his back so that the others would bow their heads too.

"Is there anything else you wished to say to me?" she said. "I do not mean to be short with you, Rhys, but I have much to see to."

"I do not want to steal your time, *mara*, but may I ask something?"

She seemed amused by his asking this, and she nodded. "Though I warn you, I may not answer."

He grinned. "May we walk today? We would all like a few moments of air." When she hesitated, he said, "I know this is a large question. Please, I am sorry if I offended you."

She shook her head. "No, no, you didn't." She looked down at him again. "You may walk about the courtyard. At dusk would be safest, I think," she said to Yaro over her shoulder.

Yaro nodded. "I will see to it."

"It will not be for much longer," she told Rhys. "But for now, it is best that few see you."

"I understand. And thank you, *mara*. You are very kind to us." He couldn't resist noting, "There are many more in Karak today."

"Yes."

"Forgive me for asking, *mara*, but has something happened?" Rhys said, avoiding Yaro's scowl.

The queen's look was hard to read as she gazed

down upon him. Her demeanor certainly changed, but he couldn't quite put his finger on it.

"Yes, little *plarra*. We are going to war."

He stood there with his mouth agape. He didn't know why he thought this wasn't coming— of course it was. General Hammond thought of nothing else. She was champing at the bit. But somehow, deep down, Rhys hoped they might have adverted all-out war. It was a pipe dream, he knew that, but it hadn't been more so than in that moment.

She leaned down so that only he could hear her say, "I am sorry for it. Truly."

He was able to nod, and she then took her leave.

Turning around, he beheld the others of the group looking at him, expectantly awaiting a full translation of everything. Cara was the first to notice his deflated face.

"Rhys, what's wrong?"

———

To keep herself from fidgeting, Elena bit her tongue and would have made it bleed if two officers hadn't walked in. She tried to swallow as she watched them take a seat across the chrome table from her, but her throat wouldn't work.

The two officers, a stout man with a scraggly beard and a lean woman with an angled bob, asked if she wanted more water. Elena jerkily shook her head, desperately wanting them to find their files more quickly.

This wasn't Elena's first debriefing. Having gone on that disastrous delegation, she had of course been asked to recount all she could remember. It was routine. That's how the military worked.

Her sickening anxiety spawned from more than just her intense dislike of being caged in metal boxes—she had had enough of that on the journey here. Because this wasn't her first time, she knew what was coming, and she knew not to look forward to it. Questions had to be answered the right way. She had to keep her story straight.

It wasn't that she necessarily wanted or was planning on lying to the regime. As a soldier there was something inherently wrong to her about not finishing the job, and that included reporting back. But she knew better than to believe she could spill her guts and not expect to have a healthy amount of suspicion cast upon her.

The truth was, she didn't like the regime's policy on the natives. Even during her time aboard ship, Elena hadn't been a big fan of General Hammond, and she hadn't made up that ground on Terra Nova. When she guarded their former native prisoner—whom she called Steve but Rhys said was named Yaro—she found herself kind of liking him. He was a kindred spirit of sorts. And her time with Rhys in Karak, while less than ideal, hadn't been all terrible. There was a whole world beyond the perimeter of New Haven, one the general was desperate to keep them away from.

"All right then, Ames, I'm Lt. Krauss," said

the man, "and this is Lt. Colonel Sulla. Let's get started."

"Where'd you want me to start?"

"With the general terrain, if you would."

Elena cleared her throat. She kept her syllables short, trying to move as little as possible when speaking. She recounted the plains, the desert, and the treacherous strait they had to cross, then described the Tikshi's jungle subcontinent.

They asked her about the Tikshi themselves, how she found them and their domain.

Here she edited. She described the Tikshi, how they looked, how they moved, what their houses looked like. She confirmed that the picture they showed her was indeed the Tikshi leader, Treya. She didn't, however, tell them her thoughts on the Tikshi.

She actually didn't have too many. She felt, though, that agreeing to an alliance wasn't a good idea. The Tikshi had been at war with the Charneki for what sounded like centuries. The humans were out of their depth, stepping into this preexisting world war. Not exactly what the fledgling colonies needed. But she kept that to herself.

Krauss was nodding. "Good. Now, we'd appreciate your account of the two exchanges with Charneki hostiles."

"Nothing much to say, really. They were both ambushes, one in the foothills, one in the canyons. They were dealt with, and we moved on."

"C'mon now, don't be coy."

Elena nearly jumped out of her skin at the sound of General Hammond's voice. She had walked into the small room without making a sound and stood in front of the closed door, her hands neatly folded behind her. Krauss and Sulla had the tact to salute.

General Hammond's eyes took their sweet time looking at the three of them in the room before she pulled up the last chair, sitting on the other side of Krauss.

"I-I'm sorry, General, I don't—"

"At ease, soldier," she said with a sort of amused

grin playing at her lips. "All I want is a full, truthful account from you. Then you can go."

"I was giving—"

"How many hostiles did you down, soldier?"

Elena froze, her mouth open. A frown slowly crept onto her face. "I-I don't remember, ma'am."

"No?"

"It was . . . chaotic."

"I see." She brought up from her gauntlet some projected text and scrolled through it without looking down. Instead she kept eye contact with Elena. "The video feed from your speeder registered a number."

Elena was granted a space to say something, but she stayed silent, her jaws clamped shut. Her insides felt like someone had a hand in her and was trying to pull them all out.

"Two." The general scrolled through Elena's profile. "Correct me if I'm wrong, but it says here that you're in the top percentile of marksmen. I have your commanding officer going on record saying you're the best shot in her platoon, maybe even my whole armed forces. Now, what I can't make sense of is why my best gunner killed two native hostiles when, armed with a sixty-six automatic, she could have taken down quadruple that number in five seconds."

"I-I . . ."

Unprepared for this, Elena stared at the empty space between Krauss and Sulla, who looked almost as helpless as she felt. She should have known, should have seen this coming. The expedition south had been a test. And she failed.

General Hammond was waiting, leaning back in her chair slightly. Elena had the nauseating feeling that the general could just smell the kill.

"I was dazed, ma'am," she finally said. "My driver got shot, and I had to patch him up."

"Your replacement driver, if I remember Klein's report."

"Yes."

"A friend of yours. The engineer, O'Callahan."

She could feel her pulse throbbing in her neck, head, and hands. "Yes."

"Funny how that name keeps coming up."

Elena couldn't help it; she met General Hammond's gaze. She realized she was being played with.

Folding her hands on the table before her, General Hammond leaned forward. "Do you know what I think, Ames?"

She wasn't stupid enough to answer.

"There's a reason ninety-three percent of your shots were non-fatal. Do you know that reason?"

"Off day?"

She really did jump when the general's hand slammed on the table. Elena, Krauss, and Sulla looked up, terrified, as the general smiled serenely at them.

"I just have a few more questions for you, Ames." This time she did look down at her gauntlet as she brought up a series of images. "This is quite simple. I'm going to show you some natives. I want you to identify them."

She bit her lip again. There was a glint in the general's eyes, and Elena knew there were right and wrong answers.

The first image was of two tall Charneki warriors standing together talking. The one on the right she immediately recognized as Steve.

"Now I know it might take a moment since it's been some time since your visit to their city, but I want you to think long and hard. Tell me who these two are."

"What does it matter?"

One side of the general's mouth inched up. "Start with the one on the right."

Wetting her lips, Elena had to say, "That's the warrior we had here. He's called Yaro."

"Mm. And the one on the left?"

Elena really did have to think about that. She knew she had seen him. He was the young warrior who had come to meet them when they parked on the bluffs overlooking the bay the mountain-city stood in the middle of. Through some coaxing, Rhys had discovered he was named Ondra.

She told the general this.

"And what's their relationship to the queen?"

"I don't know, ma'am."

"You can do better, Ames."

"I wasn't outside the dungeon much, I didn't—"

"Were they important to her?"

"I don't—"

"*Think*, Ames. Were they important to the queen?"

She let out a sharp breath. "Yeah, probably. I don't know. They were both there when we met the queen the second time."

General Hammond swiped across the projected screen, bringing up another picture. For a fleeting moment Elena wanted to know where in the world she had gotten these images, but she supposed Dr. Oswald had had more than a diplomatic purpose in Karak. He paid a steep price.

"This is her? Their queen."

Elena didn't know why the general needed confirmation. She sat there on a damned throne.

"Yes."

"And what's she called?"

"I don't know," Elena said, curious, underneath her terror, why the general seemed so interested. "They didn't say her name. They just called her *mara*."

"And what about the old one next to her? And the others?"

The image had been captured in the queen's throne room while she sat in state. The other Charneki wore turquoise robes.

"Rhys thought they were a counseling body," Elena said. "Like religious leaders or something."

"Very good. Now, my last question. Why you?"

"Ma'am?"

"Why did she let *you* go? Why not O'Callahan? Why not the rest?"

"I don't know."

"You expect me to believe that?"

"It's the truth! I didn't know half of what was going on—Rhys did all the talking. I was the only one there with him, so that's probably—"

"Why were only you and he brought to her a second time?"

"I don't know."

"Why, Ames?"

"I told you, I don't know! Yaro brought the two of us out and we left the rest and—"

The general leaned back in her seat. "So the big warrior, the one you had all those nice conversations with, picked you did he? Brought you up with O'Callahan."

Elena sat there, stunned.

"I'm going to say something now, Ames, and you better listen. If you want to survive in this colony, you'll decide which side you're on. I don't have time for the likes of Rhys O'Callahan. If it were up to his kind, the human race would go extinct. If you give a damn about your species' survival, you'll forget any sympathy you have towards the natives."

When Elena didn't say anything, the general continued, "I'm fighting a war here, Ames. And you're a soldier. So start acting like one, or you'll find yourself quite alone in this world. Dismissed."

It took her a moment to realize it was over, and the surge of relief almost alleviated her overwhelming dread. She stood, did a halfhearted salute, and turned from them.

Elena resisted the urge to run out of the room. She didn't stop to think about any of it until she was well away from Headquarters and walking back to her platoon's hangar.

Slowly everything that happened crept into her mind, and the ugly threat of General Hammond's words sunk in. New Haven wasn't safe—it probably never had been. They had travelled seven years to escape the cutthroat reality of Earth, but Elena knew now that they could have saved the trip. They brought that reality with them. They had let

General Hammond make Terra Nova a true new Earth.

She realized she had been standing in the middle of the road for several moments, just staring out at the white-capped mountains to the north. Suddenly her brain snapped like an elastic band, and she felt, in her heart, that she was changing. But what could she do?

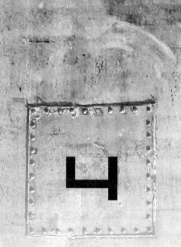

"Right, and then that goes there, and this, this goes right here," Hugh narrated as he rerouted a subfuse.

After helping Saranov maintain the starship engines, convert them to generators, and once again oversee their maintenance, Hugh felt he could do all this in his sleep. It was, however, new to the young man sitting beside him.

Keaton Myers was a pleasant person with a sunny smile. Also an apprentice on the journey over, Keaton seemed to have arrived, though seven years older, with his optimism still intact.

He did a low whistle. "Well, all I have to say is that I'm happy I didn't have to do this first."

Hugh grinned. "It's not too bad—you'll see. It was all meant to be repurposed."

"Pretty amazing, isn't it? The amount of planning this all took."

"Tell me about it. I still can't believe my apartment was once part of a starship."

"I'll be happy when construction's done," Keaton said. "I'm ready to get settled."

"You have a lot of plans?"

"Not really, aside from just getting to live. This place is better than I could've ever imagined, you know? I want to start my life here."

Hugh couldn't help almost feeling overwhelmed by Keaton's intense desire to see the start of what they had all been promised: a normal, fulfilling life, one away from the pollution and turmoil of the sunburnt Earth. It was almost ghostly, hearing Keaton's words. Hugh had had that same intense desire, though he found it hard to articulate. All he had wanted was to settle down with Rhys, become brothers again, learn how to live again. So many things were in the way of that now.

Hugh cleared his throat. There was something he meant to ask, and if he didn't get it out now, he thought he never would.

"So you don't think any more will come? We're it?"

Keaton looked up, his sunny face clouding. He swallowed hard, the little ball of his throat moving up and down.

"I think a third expedition was in the works— ours had such a quick turnover, there was hope they might get a lot more off before the solar storm hit it. We got the transmission about a year out; I doubt they had time to finish."

Hugh leaned back, putting his weight on his splayed hands. "Just like that. Did a lot of . . . ?" he couldn't finish. He hadn't found anyone's name he recognized on the second expedition's registry. They were all gone.

"Governments were handing out suicide pills even before we left," Keaton said, looking down at the specialized screwdriver in his hand. "I think most just did it that way. We think some might still be indoors, so who knows—maybe, someday they'll come."

Hugh nodded. No they wouldn't.

So that was that. His mother, everyone he had ever known on Earth was dead. Everyone except Rhys.

Keaton cleared his throat before peering under the generator. Coaxing Hugh back into work, the two of them were able to forget the circumstances of their coming to Terra Nova, losing themselves in the challenge. They did, at one point, have to lift one panel to do a quick check of the core casing. Hugh never liked that part, having to look at the white-hot atomic heart of the generator. He did it as quickly as possible.

"That should be good for today," Hugh said, wiping some sweat and grime off his forehead.

Keaton checked the time on his gauntlet. "Wanna get some dinner?"

"I'd kill for some dinner," Hugh replied.

The two of them cleaned up their station before heading out with several other engineers, taking the elevators down to ground level. It was surreal to walk out of a starship carcass again. All up and down the hull of the ship, crews cut away at premeasured strips of metal plating. Rivets the size of his arm lay strewn all over the perimeter.

Sunset crept over the new colony, which had recently been christened San Angelo. It was a sprawling tent city, more than double the size of New Haven. Already organized along the same lines as the first colony, San Angelo had four quadrants: residential, market, industrial, and administrative. The last one was the main difference; Kimura had his makeshift headquarters in the administrative quadrant, and all other official colony business went through there. In New Haven, it was the military quadrant with General Hammond's headquarters at its heart.

They made for the nearest mess tent, which thankfully wasn't too far off. Hugh's stomach growled something fierce.

Sitting down on a patch of grass with Keaton and several packs of protein bars and nutrition tabs, Hugh ripped open the first packet and began chewing.

"There's been talk around here about these natives," Keaton said.

Hugh looked over and found him watching him. He nodded.

"What're they like?"

"They don't like us much."

Keaton laughed. "I get that. But surely we can talk to them, make them understand this's our last chance."

"I don't think talking's an option anymore."

"What's that mean?"

Hugh lowered his voice when he said, "We tried it once. Didn't go so well."

"Why?"

The mouthful of protein pack when down rough and dry.

"They took the delegation prisoners. They never wanted to talk, and they might have already killed . . . " Again, he couldn't finish.

He almost didn't hear Keaton say, "That bad? We didn't think we'd be competing with another species. But then, it's selfish to think we're alone out here. What exactly are we supposed to do now? Can't anything be done for the people captured?"

Hugh shook his head absentmindedly.

"Why not?"

"It's not on General Hammond's agenda."

"Well, what is?"

"She wants war."

Keaton's brows shot up at that. "Nobody here wants to go to war. We just got here for god's sake!"

"You probably won't have much choice."

"Hugh, you really think that's the answer? You really want to go to war?"

He looked up at him, the nutrition tab tasteless in his mouth despite the burning citrus sensation on his tongue.

"My brother's one of the prisoners."

———————

The storeroom was a hive of activity, converted, once more, into a workshop. People kept dashing from the room up the steep stone steps into the courtyard above, bearing a little metal piece, a plan, or a tool.

Most of the human delegation were out of their league when it came to such technical planning, but Perry and Katja oversaw a steady flow of work, Perry supervising the production and Katja in charge of assembly.

Making the generator was proving much easier

than expected, for just two days before, the queen had brought the humans out of their storeroom into the courtyard. Standing in the middle was a dented, lifeless cruiser.

"Where did you get this?" Rhys had asked.

"Warriors from the plains recovered it," the queen replied stoically.

"But how—?"

"It is ours now. You will use it to make your generators," she had said, not looking at him.

Rhys was still troubled by the appearance of the cruiser, for it meant there was fighting beyond Karak that the queen wasn't telling him about. The cruiser caused a violent division within the delegation. Five soldiers in particular refused to have anything to do with the generator project, angry at being asked to convert this human technology into something for the natives. Those five sat in the corner of the storeroom in protest.

Reviving the cruiser's engine and turning it into a generator was easier than making a generator from scratch; still, it wasn't a popular plan. Rhys got the feeling a generator from scratch would have caused less of a stir, but they were under direct orders from the queen, and for their own survival, they needed to impress her and her council.

Rhys kept an eye on the five soldiers. Any sabotage on their part could be catastrophic for all of them.

Grinning at Cara, Rhys took the small part she had just finished polishing and headed from the storeroom. Perry and a few others, with the help of several Charneki metalworkers, had been working for almost two weeks to cut all the small pieces needed. After they came out of the fire, they were handed over to be polished, with one final measurement before Katja got her hands on them.

He crossed the narrow, railed walkway leading from the door of the storeroom to the base of the steps, nodding at the two Charneki guards on either side of the storeroom door then to the two flanking the landing. Hopping up the steps, he came into the courtyard, a circular space rimmed in bushes bearing native flowers and carpeted with bluish-green grass. The lawn was cut into four equal pieces by four paths leading into a central tiled space where a great stone basin sat, which would fill with rainfall.

Katja, several others, and about half a dozen Charneki guards stood in the courtyard, along with the stripped carcass of the cruiser. A ways off, along the colonnaded walkway leading from the courtyard, he could see more guards.

Walking up with his piece, Rhys handed it to Katja and asked how things were looking.

"Pretty good," she said. "We're on schedule."

"Always good to hear."

"Did Perry say anything about the lights?"

"He thinks he's found something that'll work. I guess when he was trying to explain wires, a Charneki pointed him towards a native vine. Turns out they can act pretty much like electrical wires, and he's hoping to test it soon."

"I'll believe it when I see it, but fingers crossed, I guess."

"What'll happen if that doesn't work?"

"We'll have to scrap a couple gauntlets for the extra wires. Not my Plan A."

Nodding, Rhys let her get back to work, and headed over to Yaro. He grinned up at the big Charneki. Rhys felt he had to compensate for the others' dampened spirits. The Charneki couldn't think they were unwilling, or worse, making a weapon.

"*Muma ger nerma sua?*" Rhys asked, 'How are you feeling today?'

"I am well," Yaro replied. "And you?"

"Pleased," he said with a smile. "The queen will like it."

Rhys looked up at him. Yaro's upper lip was twitching.

"You do not like it?"

"It is . . . different. It does not look like it will do anything."

"Not yet. Right now it is many pieces. But soon it will make light."

That didn't seem to console Yaro, who continued to regard the generator with disdain. "And how will making light help us?" he asked.

Rhys's eyebrows rose at hearing so many words out of Yaro at once. Rather taciturn, the queen's favorite warrior, at least to Rhys's knowledge, rarely said more than he had to. He didn't know if he could remember the last time he had asked a question other than, "And you?"

"If you do not wish it to be dark, then it will not be," he said, pushing through his awkward sentence structure.

"We have *buna* for that."

A native rock similar chemically to coal, *buna*, or what the humans called cerulean, was a pretty blue stone that almost looked like colored glass and produced an otherworldly blue flame. There were extensive mines of it up in the northern tundra, and when the humans took over the native villages just south of New Haven and discovered the cerulean, they hoped to use it as a fuel source. From what Rhys understood, the human mining effort had gone abysmally. He didn't know if they were still trying.

"This will be much brighter than *buna*. You could make Karak light up the whole night."

"Night is a time for darkness."

Rhys made a face at him. "You will just have to trust me."

One side of Yaro's mouth inched up. He looked around a moment and then leaned down so that only Rhys could hear him when he said, "I am glad the queen trusts you. You are an interesting little *plarra*."

He grinned. "I wish to be worthy of her trust, I promise you."

"I believe you, little one. And I also believe you want to help us, though I still do not know why."

"I like the Charneki," he said. "I do not want to see Charneki and humans fight."

Rhys's words brought on a silence that lasted several long moments. Both knew that despite Rhys's best wishes, everything was coming to a head. General Hammond had been yearning for a war, and now it seemed the queen was ready to give her one.

Maybe that made the generator futile. In a way, he supposed he was a traitor to his species. He didn't know how much he really was tipping the scales, but he had every intention of aiding them wherever he could. It wasn't just to keep him and his comrades alive—he genuinely thought, if there was to be a war, at least let it be a fairer one. The Charneki had numbers on their side, but that was a terrible failsafe that he suspected the queen liked just about as much as he did.

Still, he clung to the hope that maybe, if nothing else, these small technical innovations might act as a sort of deterrent. If the Charneki's superior numbers had kept General Hammond back, now with a whole new batch of humans, and presumably more weapons, something else was going to have to dissuade her. If Rhys could do that, if he could help make the Charneki too dangerous to attack, he hoped it might buy the opposition in New Haven enough time. General Hammond wouldn't be in charge forever, and he hoped her warmongering would go with her.

"Do you miss your home?" Yaro asked.

Rhys looked up at him in surprise, startled at such a question. In all honesty, he had been avoiding it for quite a while. He shoved his hands in his jacket pockets.

"I did not like it there."

Yaro glanced down at him, apparently astonished at that answer. "Why?"

He shrugged, avoiding Yaro's eyes.

"What about your family?"

Rhys almost shook his head but stopped, saying instead, "I do not have a family."

Yaro's hairless brows rose at this, and he suddenly looked sad. "You are alone?"

He cleared his throat. "I had a brother once."

Yaro seemed to sense his discomfort and said nothing, though Rhys could still feel his eyes on him. Rhys was relieved; he didn't know how he could convey to Yaro the pain of going to sleep knowing he had a twin, then waking up seemingly several moments later to have a grownup stranger telling him he was Hugh now.

He glared down at the ground, his fists clenched as he willed the tears to stay behind his eyes. Everyone acted like it was only hard for Hugh— he saw it in their faces, Elena's, Cass's, Saranov's; but the truth was that Rhys's reality had shattered in a moment, and he was expected to just accept it. Nobody cared that the brother he knew, the brother he loved, was gone. It wasn't the same Hugh looking down at him. His partner-in-crime, his accomplice, his best friend had just vanished into thin air. So yes, Rhys was alone, except for a few short, precious weeks when Zaynab had filled that hole in him.

Did he miss his home? No, he couldn't, for he didn't have one. Did he miss Hugh? No, how could he? That man was barely better than a stranger. Did he miss his brother? Desperately.

"Perhaps it is good you found your way to the queen." Yaro's voice snapped him back, and Rhys looked up to find Yaro peering down at him meaningfully. "She is also alone."

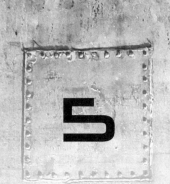

5

Zeneba's breath caught when Rhys nodded at her, signaling that it was ready.

She whispered to Yaro quietly, and he brought his metal spear down, the sound cutting through the curious chatter. This brought the council to attention.

"My fine council," she said, "the time has come to see what the demons have made for us. I ask you for your patience and your open mind." Looking at Rhys, she said, "Please, Rhys, show them what you have done."

Zeneba wasn't quite prepared for the way her stomach twisted in knots. She desperately needed this to succeed—her council hadn't always been on her side after she announced her desire to banish one of her former tutors, Elder Vasya. He had never supported her reign, and during her cycle of mourning for Zaynab, he ruled the council. She suspected that he coveted her seat. He left Karak after her claim that he was a blasphemer and hadn't been seen since.

She knew she stood to lose almost as much as her human captives with this generator. Their making of medicines had been a sort of pet project of hers, supported by a few, but that support had withered away upon the discovery and execution of the human spy. She needed it back if she wanted to continue indulging her projects with Rhys.

All looked to Rhys and the two human metal-workers who stood before her dais. The generator certainly was an odd-looking thing, an amalgamation of metal pieces and parts, with several tendrils of *jant'a* vines running from it to a series of glass bulbs.

She and Rhys shared an apprehensive, excited look as the female metalworker stepped forward and pressed her finger against a small circular red piece.

Instantly the bulbs flickered then bright white light blasted through the hall.

Zeneba beamed through her watering eyes, reminding herself that Rhys had told her not to look directly at the light. She had seen the generator make light the previous day, and a great weight lifted from her shoulders at seeing it again. She understood the humans weren't happy to make the generator out of their vehicle, but it was a necessary test of their dependability.

The hall filled with almost deafening noise as her council gasped and cried out in astonishment. Those further back craned their necks, and those closer clamored for a better look at the light-maker.

"Nahara on high . . ."

Zeneba looked over and caught the Skywatcher staring at the light, his eyes rimmed in tears. She put a hand on his shoulder, asked him if he was all right.

"I-I can see it. I can see their light."

Her eyes widened. "Truly, Wise One?"

He nodded, wiping at his eyes. "It pierces the darkness."

She couldn't contain her smile and had the overwhelming desire to put her arms around the wizened Elder. She refrained, knowing such things weren't done, but still she was touched to witness the happiness on his face at seeing something.

He placed a hand on Zeneba's and said, "I cannot help feeling it is a sign, Golden One. It is no mistake I see Nahara again."

Those closest to the dais had heard, and the news quickly spread through the hall.

Her heart swelling with Elder Zhora's words, Zeneba stood, a smile still on her face. The council bowed their heads.

"I share the Skywatcher's feelings—this cannot

be a mistake. We have been gifted an opportunity, and we must seize it."

"It is very impressive," said Elder Ha, stepping forward, "but, Golden One, what can we honestly do with such a thing? With war coming, do you want to use up precious metal?"

"I understand your hesitation, Wise One. It is a great leap we are taking, but I feel we must jump. There is, in fact, a way these light-makers might aid us. Ondra," she said, turning to look at him where he stood, several paces from her dais, "please tell my council the report you received from Chieftain Samuka just this morning."

Bowing his head to her, Ondra addressed the council: "Reports have come that the Tikshi have been building a great many ships. The Chieftain believes, when they attack, they will do so by water."

Zeneba couldn't help noting the lack of enthusiasm in Ondra's voice and the way his mouth was downturned during his speech. She didn't know why she found it odd, but she couldn't consider it more, for Elder Jeska stepped forward.

"Please, Golden One, what does this have to do with the light-maker?"

She nodded at the Elder, acknowledging she heard his question, but looked at Rhys when she said, "Tell me, little *plarra*, can your generator make a light many times larger than this one?"

Rhys spoke quickly with the two metalworkers before answering, "Yes, *mara*. We can make you larger light and, if you wish, more generators."

"Very good. Now, we suspect the Tikshi will come from the southern sea. We also know it is the Tikshi way to attack at night. What I propose to you is that we build many great lights, place them all around the bay, even send them to cities along the coast if there is time. If we can do this, we may just take away their element of surprise and be prepared for them when they come, for, Wise Ones, they *will* come to Karak."

The Red Hall was silent, and Zeneba tried to

hide her anxiousness as she watched the faces of her council. They looked amongst themselves, but no one uttered a word.

It was Elder Ha who spoke first. "Please, Golden One, if the Tikshi are coming, would it not be better to have the humans make us weapons?"

Zeneba's eyes flicked to Rhys, and she saw how markedly paler he looked. She nodded at him. "Tell them what you have told me."

"We cannot make you *guns*," he said, using his human word. "We do not have the people for it."

"How can you be believed?" asked Elder Ha, his eyes suspicious.

Rhys took a moment, searching for the right words. "You have healers for the sick, smiths for metal. So we have makers for weapons. None of us here are makers, only scholars and warriors."

"But you built these generators!" cried an Elder from the back.

"We had an *engine* to build it from," said Rhys,

glancing at Zeneba. "We may make more by copying this one."

"Then copy your weapons!"

"We did not come into Karak with weapons," Rhys said. "We were not allowed to."

Zeneba raised her hand, proud of Rhys for defending himself. She understood such weapons would certainly aid their war effort. However, even if the humans were lying and they could build them, that didn't mean they would. Zeneba would be expected to offer an ultimatum, weapons for their lives, and she knew they would refuse, either from lack of ability or willingness. She couldn't put them to the sword now.

"We have in these generators a compromise," she said. "If it is the will of the council, I will negotiate with the humans for more of their technology." She looked down at Rhys. "But for now, we must accept this gift and put it to use."

It was Elder Plia who spoke first, and he said with a wide smile, "So says our *mara*!"

"So says our *mara!*" the others chanted, bowering their heads.

She had to stop her cry of triumph. She glanced over her shoulder at the Skywatcher and felt warmed by his proud look. Yaro wore a similar one, and she nodded at him, her face aglow in her success.

"Let us meet our enemy with the fire of Nahara herself!" she said.

Her spirits were almost dampened when she looked over at Ondra and found him with a wary look. He didn't realize she gazed at him, and she stared perhaps too long, for his expression worried her. She would speak with him later—though, she had already intended that.

She found her smile again when she met Rhys's eyes and they shared in the triumph together. The two metalworkers looked understandably relieved.

Zeneba watched as several curious Elders came up to speak to Rhys, and through him they asked the metalworkers questions about the generator.

She smiled to see his enthusiastic face, and all at once it struck her—Rhys reminded her of Zaynab.

Stepping lightly off her dais, she used the general excitement to slip over to Ondra. He looked about to see if anyone was watching, casting a wary look in Yaro's direction.

"Meet me in the Blue Garden after," she whispered with an impish grin.

One side of his mouth rose, his color shifting to a rich, pleased gold. He nodded.

She moved away from him then, walking into the pack that had amassed around the humans. Once she touched the shoulder of the nearest Elder, they moved for her so that she could approach Rhys.

"You have done well, little *plarra*."

He bowed to her. "I hope it pleases you, *mara*."

She leaned down and said, "Your idea may very well save many Charneki lives. For that I thank you," she looked at the two metalworkers, "all of you."

The other two bowed their heads once Rhys had translated for them.

Once Zeneba had arranged a committee, headed by Elder Plia, who seemed most interested and moved by the generators, to oversee the continuing production of light-makers, she declared the meeting at an end.

Elder Zhora rose to follow the others out of the Red Hall but paused to say to her, "Nahara smiles upon you, Golden One. You were never more the *mara* she intended you to be than you are today."

Touched beyond measure by his words, she replied, "You honor me, Skywatcher. But you know I could not have gotten here without you."

"I am so very proud of you."

She took his hands and squeezed them.

With one last smile he hobbled out of the hall so that it was just a few of them left.

Zeneba and Ondra exchanged glances as he walked with several others of the Guard towards the entrance. She suddenly itched to leave herself.

Turning around, she caught Yaro watching her. She gave him her best disarming smile.

"I don't think it could have gone any better," she said.

Stepping off the dais, Yaro replied, "I am pleased you stood your ground. I trust you to lead us forward."

She let herself slip into a shimmering gold to show Yaro how much his words meant to her.

"There is much work to be done," she told Rhys, "but I have faith you will rise to the challenge."

He grinned up at her. "You honor us."

"Yaro will take you back. You must tell the others the good news."

He bowed, and the others followed him. When they straightened, the two metalworkers went to either side of the generator and lifted up the panel of *unta* bark it sat on.

Picking up his spear, Yaro gestured for the humans to follow him out.

Zeneba was left alone in the hall. She gave them

a bit of a head start before leaving the hall herself. Ankha, her caretaker since she first came to Karak, stood just outside.

"I heard the news!" she said excitedly as she held out her hands to collect Zeneba's copious ornaments.

"Oh, Ankha, I have such high hopes for this! I like to think it proves that we might have peace someday."

"What do you mean?" she asked.

Zeneba placed the *lahn-nahar*, the two jade gauntlets and gold chain with a jade medallion that served as vestiges of her power, on the purple cushion Ankha held. She added to them her three rings and gold circlet.

"Well, we certainly can't kill all the demons, Ankha. But if we can work with them like we have here, then we might just be able to live in peace with them once the war is over."

Ankha smiled, turning a rosy gold. "I had not thought of that, *mara*. I hope you are right."

Zeneba continued pulling jewelry and her fine outer robes off, and Ankha gave her a look.

"All of it? Now? Couldn't we—?"

"I'm sorry—I have to be somewhere."

Ankha looked her up and down. "Wearing so little?"

"If anyone inquires, tell them I'm up in the Cloud Gardens," she said, pulling the delicate filigree off of her headdress, a natural crown of skin and bone all female Charneki grew.

"Where will you be really?" asked Ankha suspiciously.

Zeneba grinned. "I'm not telling you—Yaro would get it out of you, and I can't have that."

Ankha looked aghast, so Zeneba trotted off before she could ask any more questions. She knew Ankha couldn't follow laden with all that jewelry.

Her excitement quickening her step, Zeneba made for one of the smaller gardens towards the back of the palace. It was one of her favorites, though she rarely got to go. It was a private little space, few venturing around that far.

Ondra was already there when she arrived, and he smiled to see her, flashing gold. She hadn't seen him much at all amid the chaos of recent days, so she counted herself lucky she had been able to arrange this.

Though they were open with each other now about their love, it was still a secret from others. A *mar* or *mara* wasn't free to pledge themselves to one, but instead was expected to devote themselves, a child of Nahara and Undin, to all Charneki. They especially had to keep it from Yaro who, while he seemed to be coming around to Ondra, certainly wouldn't approve.

"You're full of schemes today," he said, coming to her. He took her wrists in his hands. "You were masterful in there."

She grinned to conceal her blush. "Well, thank you. I have my moments."

Pulling away before he got too many ideas,

Zeneba strode over to a stone bench and pulled two broad Charneki blades from underneath. Brandishing one, she handed Ondra, who wore a rather baffled expression, the other.

"I'm afraid I'm quite out of practice," she said, "but with war coming, I should probably sharpen my skills, wouldn't you say?"

He regarded her skeptically, knowing better than to insult her by saying she needed practice.

"Hadn't you thought to ask Yaro? He taught you before."

She made a face. "Well if you want me to, I'll go find him."

He grabbed her wrist. "No, no."

"Well then." She took her stance.

She had almost forgotten how much she liked sparring, how much she reveled in getting to stretch and work her muscles. Loving the feel of the lunge, the parry, the thrust, she laughed giddily as she jumped up onto the bench, defending herself from a quick jab.

"Not so fast!"

She couldn't get away from him as he wrapped an arm around her middle, and they stumbled together into a *lanza* bush. They shimmered gold in the setting sunlight, laughing like they were children again.

"Do you concede?" she said, leaning back to look at him.

He grinned. "I know when I'm beaten."

She wasn't ready for him touching his mouth to her forehead, and for a moment she forgot to breathe.

"I thought we said . . ."

"Yes, sorry, I—" he cleared his throat. "I forgot myself."

Zeneba touched a hand to his shoulder. "I didn't think it would be so hard."

Nodding, he said, "I'm sorry—I don't want to burden you. You have enough to contend with."

His dampened tone saddened her, and she said quickly, "No, Ondra, that isn't it." She took his wrists. "You make me happy, and I don't think I can make you understand how much it means to me to feel that way again. I want you in my life—I want this to work somehow, but . . . we can't get carried away. Now just isn't our time."

"But our time will come?"

She smiled up at him. "I hope so."

He seemed contented with that, returning her smile. "Is there something I can do for you?" he asked. "Something that would help?"

"Yes, actually," she said. "I'd like you to help Yaro oversee this project. I know he would do it all, but the clans are due soon and we will need to start holding official meetings—what?" She stopped when she saw his face dropping.

"I'd rather Yaro keep his current task," he said.

"What does that mean?"

"You really want me to help these demons?"

Her mouth fell open. "How could you say that?"

"Please, no, Zeneba, that's not . . . " He put a

hand over his heart as she took several steps back. "I just don't trust them."

"Still? Ondra, what more can they do?"

"They'll do anything to stay alive! Can't you see that? Why should we trust them? You gave them your warning—yet still they slaughter us. I'm sorry, I thought I could stay silent, but . . . "

"This is what I want to do, Ondra. Why can't you support me?"

"Zeneba, I would walk to the Sunlit Realm and back for you—you know that!"

"But I don't understand why you still resist their help. If you don't trust them . . . it's like you don't trust me."

"You know that's not true. But I'm a warrior, and they are the enemy."

Straightening, Zeneba tried to look past her hurt feelings to do what Elder Zhora had taught her: see the middle.

"You will help with this project," she said, holding her hand up to keep him from speaking. "You will work alongside them, speak with them, and after you've done this, if you still feel the same, you can have nothing more to do with them or my plan."

Ondra bowed stiffly. "As you wish."

He made to move away, but she reached out a hand. "I'm asking this as me, Zeneba, not your *mara*. I need your support, Ondra—I need you to see what I see."

He searched her eyes for a long moment before finally nodding slowly. "Only for you."

She touched her hand to the side of his face. "It's faint, but I feel as if I see the future, just beyond the horizon. There will be life after this war, I just know it."

6

Those summoned to the meeting room milled about, talking quietly in small groups, but Hugh could see in their eyes they were nervous. The command had come to his gauntlet just that morning bearing a classified ID number. Only one woman could issue such a command.

He stood in a corner with Cass while Saranov and a few other engineers stood close by. The best of the industrial and science quadrants were in that room.

"What could she want?" Cass murmured under her breath.

Hugh knew she didn't need an answer, just wanting to get the nervous energy out somehow. He glanced down at her and saw she gnawed on her thumb nail. He put a hand on her shoulder.

The general didn't keep them waiting much longer, walking in with an imperious face. She folded her hands behind her back as her presence caused a hush throughout the room.

"Thank you for coming," she said, gazing out at them without actually looking at one particular person. "I've something to discuss with you that might very well save this colony."

Some shifted their weight, others looked around at those nearest them, but no one was foolish enough to respond to such a statement.

"I won't bore you with the particulars, but I can confirm we will be going to war soon. The native threat is growing, and we must combat it. With our alliance to the Tikshi secured, we have the numbers to take on this task, but I want more than that. That's where you come in. We are the last humans in the universe, and I don't want to see a massacre if we can avoid it. Human life is too precious. That's why you will build me a failsafe."

This caused several mutters, and the group looked at her in surprise. Hugh's heart raced in his chest.

"You want us to build a weapon," Saranov finally said.

The general's gaze flicked to him. Her lips pursed. "A bomb, to be exact, yes. Something big enough to take out their capital city if plans don't go right. An atomic generator can be dismantled and converted. That should do nicely, I think."

The engineers and scientists stood there in stunned silence. Surely she wasn't suggesting . . . ? Couldn't she remember what nuclear warfare had accomplished back on Earth?

"We can't build a nuclear weapon!" said another engineer.

"Can't," her eyes flicked to him, "or won't?"

"Shutting down a generator to make a bomb won't look good."

Everyone held their breath, glancing Saranov's way. It wasn't that he spoke the truth, it was that the truth wasn't what the general wanted to hear. Saranov had already gotten himself on the general's bad side more than once, and it scared Hugh to wonder how much more he would get away with.

General Hammond, though, didn't seem affected by his words. "And what would you suggest?"

Saranov looked around at the others assembled before saying, "We can still make you what you want—it'll just take time."

She stood there considering, and Hugh knew she understood what Saranov was really getting at just as much as he and the others did. Saranov was stalling. It would be relatively easy—time consuming but easy—to convert a subordinate generator into an atomic bomb. To construct a different kind of weapon from scratch certainly would take more time and resources.

Saranov played his hand now; she could threaten them if they didn't make the atomic bomb, but then she would almost certainly have a public outcry she couldn't suppress on her hands. Not only this, but, while she could have them killed for not following orders, she would then be left without anyone to make her bomb, atomic or no. It was a tightrope Saranov walked, and the others would have to follow him.

Hugh couldn't say how relieved and surprised he felt when she didn't call Saranov's bluff, saying, "Fine, then. Have it your way. But I will have this done. The colony must survive." She looked at each of them in turn before stopping at Saranov to say, "I expect plans within the week. You'll begin construction then. Mark me, I strongly advise against any . . . other ideas. This war is coming. You might be the only people standing in the way of humanity's destruction. Think on that. Dismissed."

Hugh and Cass exchanged shell-shocked looks before following the others out of the sparse meeting room. He stared at the back of Saranov's head as they walked down the narrow corridor back out into the military quadrant, and all he could think was that Rhys was in that native city. General Hammond asked him to drop a bomb on his own brother.

———————

Elena drummed her fingers on the table, resisting the urge to check the time on her gauntlet again. It wasn't like Cass to be late.

Picking up her cup, she sipped the last drops of carbonated water and started chewing the ice. The people sitting close by looked over at her. She gave them her best sneer.

She didn't like being left alone these days.

She hated admitting it, but General Hammond's interrogation shook her to the core. Nowhere felt safe anymore, and she couldn't stand it. She was a soldier for god's sake—she should feel safe and secure in her own damned skin. Instead . . .

She looked around for Cass again.

Elena took a relieved breath when her friend finally rounded the corner, hurrying over and sitting down across from her. Her smile, however, died before even getting started when she saw Cass's face.

Solemn, Cass took several glances around before finally looking at Elena. Her shoulders were drawn in, her mouth a grim line.

"What's happened?"

"Sorry I'm late, I . . . "

Elena's eyes widened to see Cass's hands shaking. "Cass, what's . . . ?" She couldn't finish. She was so horrified to see her friend, always so bubbly and buoyant of spirit, quivering.

Cass looked up from her hands suddenly, an

unnerving smile that didn't reach her eyes settling on her mouth. "Hugh says to say 'hi' but that he can't come."

"I'm not worried about Hugh right now. I'm worried about you. What's going on?"

"I'm fine. Really I just . . . had some bad news. That's all."

Elena looked around then leaned in so that only Cass could hear her ask, "Did you hear something about the delegation? Has something happened to them?"

"No, nothing like that, it's . . . I can't . . . "

Elena saw it coming before it happened and, without thinking, without considering how much she hated touching, she threw her arms around Cass as she broke out into sobs. Cass clutched at her, repeating her name and apologizing.

"I can't, I can't," she said again and again.

"Can't do what?" Elena murmured in her ear. "Cass, you have to talk to me. You have to tell me what's going on."

Cass leaned back slightly so that they could look at each other. "I can't—you're being monitored already—I can't—I can't endanger you!"

"Endanger me! Cass, what in the world?"

Her gaze wandered to a couple sitting two tables away, and Elena suddenly realized how this must all look. Wrapping an arm around Cass, she muttered a few words and pulled her up. Supporting her, Elena led them from the restaurant over to a corner of the square where several unused benches stood.

Sitting Cass down, Elena said, "Now what's this all about?"

Cass just shook her head, hiding her face in her hands.

"Are you in trouble?"

She shook her head again.

"Do you need help? You know I don't have a qualm about punching someone if they really deserve it."

"No, thanks, that won't help," she said through

a gurgling sound in the back of her throat. Cass took a deep breath, wiped at her face, and raised her head. Her damp, puffy skin glistened in the soft light of the night-lamps.

Sitting down next to her, Elena said, "Cass, you have to tell me."

Cass's face scrunched up again and for a moment it looked as if she would descend into tears again. Sucking in a breath, she held them back long enough to say, "I-I've been asked—" she looked up at the sky "—ordered to do something, and I . . . I don't think I can."

Elena's jaw set. "The general?"

Cass looked at her then glanced down at the gauntlet Elena wore. No one knew exactly how extensively the general had the gauntlets and readers hacked; what they did know was that she could tell when they were taken off.

"It's something terrible, something unforgiveable."

"Can't you refuse?"

She shook her head.

"Now you're really worrying me."

Cass wiped at her face again. "I'm sorry, I didn't mean for . . . "

Elena sighed, resting her elbows on her knees and folding her hands before her face. The pit of her stomach twisted in a fiery knot. How dare anyone make Cass cry? How dare anyone threaten her friend? For a few moments she was thankful that Cass wasn't up to talking, for she suspected words would fail her.

They both looked up at the sound of approaching footsteps. Elena's apprehension that it was Hugh and this was going to start all over again dissipated when she saw Ulysses Carter's face. An outspoken advocate for reform, Carter was number one on General Hammond's undesirable list. She would have sent him on the doomed delegation if she could have, but there hadn't been a reason to send civilians other than Rhys.

A tall man with dark skin and eyes, Carter had

been one of the few survivors of the *Victoria*, the starship they lost mid-flight. No one who witnessed that could forget it. Elena envied the sleepers; they had all been asleep and couldn't witness that white flash consume a whole starship and leave only a cloud of brown dust.

Carter was technically a medical officer, but he had forsaken the military-supervised position in favor of more humble, civilian work. General Hammond liked to think of him as a rabble-rouser, a title he happily adopted. He affectionately called those who had attended the public forums his rabble. The forums were a thing of the past now, though, suppressed while Elena and Hugh had been south.

"Evening," he said with a nod. He looked at Elena for a moment, his eyes slightly narrowed with thought, before turning to Cass. "Would you like to get a drink later?"

Elena frowned, her mouth opening to tell him to buzz off, when Cass answered, "What time?"

"Eight."

She nodded. He grinned. He left.

Elena sat there befuddled. The last time she checked the clock it was past eight o'clock. It had to be approaching nine by now.

Cass waited until Carter was out of sight before turning to face Elena.

She looked at her expectantly.

"You know who that was?" she whispered.

"Of course I know who that was," Elena said. "What I want to know is—"

Cass put up a hand, silencing her. She then wiped at her face again until everything was dry. Smoothing over her hair, she said, "I gotta go."

Elena stood up with her. "Where?"

Cass looked around. "To get drinks."

"You're not serious."

Cass came close, wrapped her arms around her. "Now's not the time," she said. "Not yet. You know you're being monitored, and I can't endanger you or the opposition. Soon though, okay? Soon we'll come to you, and I hope you'll help us."

Elena's mouth fell open as Cass leaned back.

Cass smiled. "I'll make this all up to you, okay? I promise!"

And then she was away, a small bounce in her step again. Elena decided to take it as a good sign, though she couldn't help feeling it was more of an omen. All the mystery covered up the simple fact that Cass had found her way to Carter's opposition.

Elena sat back down. Cass. In the opposition. She had to think about it for a while, but when she did, she supposed it made sense.

Her eyes following the path Cass had taken from the square, Elena hoped with all her heart she knew what she was doing.

7

Zeneba tried not to smile as she watched Ankha bustle around her, gathering up this jewel, that brooch, a suitable robe. After Ankha placed everything out on the stand before her, Zeneba chose red and purple pieces and her crimson robe to wear over golden wrappings, a ribbon of cloth that wound round her upper chest, finally secured by a brooch shaped like an *utma* flower.

The horns bellowed from deep within the mountain, making the floor rumble. This time Zeneba did smile, and she stood up quickly, adjusting her robe on her slim shoulders, and made to leave.

Ankha followed behind, protesting that she wasn't quite finished, and continued placing the small pieces of filigree on Zeneba's headdress while they went.

As she walked down the colonnaded pathway out from her private section of the palace, she looked across the bay. All along the cliff face that bound in the bay that encircled Karak, great timber columns speared the skyline, the emblem and colors of the clans amassing behind it standing tall to greet Nahara and Undin.

She stopped for a moment, Ankha nearly running into her from behind.

"So many have come," she said in wonder.

"Of course they did," Ankha replied, securing the last filigree. "Any Charneki would answer the call of their *mara*."

Zeneba's eyes threatened to well with tears.

Ankha took her face in her hands and smiled warmly. "The people love you, Golden One. They love you and they will follow you anywhere you may lead."

Ankha wiped away Zeneba's tears as they escaped her eyes, and they stood smiling at one another.

"I hope I am worthy of them."

"None of that," Ankha said. "You will be a *mara* of legend before your days are done."

Zeneba took in a long breath, letting Ankha's fine words wash over her. She nodded, grinned, and embraced Ankha. The caretaker was rigid in her arms, surprised, and Zeneba let her go before long to avoid Ankha's favorite words of "A *mara* should not do such things."

Her robes billowing out behind her in the soft spring breeze, Zeneba marveled at all the standards set up along the cliffs. By the look of it, all the clans were represented.

She came to the landing of the great staircase, and many were there already to greet her. Elders Plia and Jeska greeted her as their Golden One, telling her what an auspicious day it was. She took the hand Elder Zhora offered her, and he whispered words of encouragement. Yaro bowed his head to her, and she smiled at him. She caught the gaze of Ondra, and they shared a look between them which Zeneba didn't know how to interpret.

He had done the duty asked of him without further complaint, but Zeneba wasn't sure if his attitude had changed. From his slight sulk she doubted it. It frustrated her that they couldn't agree. It was more than her dislike of arguing with him; Ondra had been her friend since they were small *mahiim*. His doubt gnawed at her like few things could. But she had other things at present to think on, and she wouldn't let his sour look ruin this for her.

The horns of Oria, the city along the southern strip of sand across the bay, announced that the clan leaders and their best warriors were at the waterline. Ships and *garans* bore them across the crystalline waters, and soon the clans marched up the length of Karak, seven abreast. When they stood before their *mara,* they were so great in number that they spilled out from the great staircase past the palace wall.

Raising a cry, they greeted and honored her in unison, knocking their great spears against their shields and breastplates.

For a moment there was silence, all looking at the *mara,* and the *mara* gazing down at them.

"I cannot express the joy I feel when I see all of you here," she said, her voice carrying down even to the harbor. "I am proud, for in your faces I see the future of all Charneki. These have been troubling times—the danger we face our ancestors could not begin to imagine. But I know we will rise now; we will take our place among the ancestors in the annals of our history. We will face this danger and overcome it. I will happily carve our great victory in the very walls of this city so that our children, our children's children, and all Charneki to come may look upon us and aspire to the courage, bravery, and valor of us today!"

A great cheer rang out, making Zeneba's heart swell.

"I know the task I set before you is a perilous one. I know we face a threat we have never seen before. But I also know we will meet them in battle; we will show them whose world this is, and we will show them what it is to be Charneki!"

The Brave Ones thumped their spears on the ground and chanted, "Our *mara* leads us on, our *mara* sees us through!"

"My heart is full, and I will defend you and our home to the last. We fight for our place in this world. There is much to be done, much to prepare, but when the path is underfoot, I swear to you, by those who have come before and those who are yet to be, I ride with you, I fight with you, I triumph with you!"

The mountain itself rumbled with pride at Zeneba's words, and she watched as the crowd flashed gold, shimmering under the light of the Sunned Ones, who shone bright and full down upon them.

Raising a hand, Zeneba proclaimed, "Soon we ride to face our enemy, and we will strike where it hurts. While there are more demons now, their new city is a weakness. They are ill-prepared, and that is where we will make our presence known. We will divide them, and we will defeat them. We will strike until they can stand no longer. We will reclaim our home! On then! On to the north!"

"Our *mara* leads us on!"

———————

Elena stepped back from the speeder, happy to see it shine. It was good to have it back in the Vanguard Platoon's hangar, her official reassignment having come in the day before.

It felt good to be getting back to where she belonged, with Sgt. White. There was a sense of normalcy to it. The sergeant was about the closest thing Elena had ever had to a parent, for she had been serving with her, with short interludes now and again, since she was twelve years old.

She doubted, though, that this feeling of normalcy was real. Things were changing. She could feel it everywhere in the colony; people were growing restless. There was hushed talk in the city square, in the restaurants, in the businesses. The clock was ticking on General Hammond's time; soon she would have little to no support aside from the military.

The general's grip on power seemed to be loosening, and none felt it more than Hammond herself. She proved it every time she tried quashing the opposition. More than a few members had found themselves in prison, and one had even been beaten in the square at the heart of the residential quadrant.

The military was really all she seemed to need. They had all the weapons, all the material. They could hold out against a civilian mob, barricade a few hangars. But what for? To kill the last surviving humans? That didn't sit well with Elena.

As she looked over her speeder, checking for any less than shiny spots, she began to wonder how much support General Hammond had in the military. True, it was a majority. But Elena found herself thinking that even a minority of soldiers turning against her might shorten, even undermine, any campaign against the civilians.

She knew that was treason talk. But hadn't the general committed treason against them? She made war when there should be peace, wanted death when this was their only chance at life.

Stretching out her back muscles, Elena decided to put these thoughts away for now. It wasn't the time. Not yet. But it was coming.

"You're still alive."

Turning on her heels, Elena held in her groan at the sight of Oscar Livermore. If Sgt. White was a sort of mother to Elena, then Oscar would have to be a sort of brother. But she hated the idea. One of the few cases of a mentor having two apprentices, Oscar and Elena had both been under Sgt. White during the expedition, though he was assigned and Elena chosen. The significance of this wasn't lost on either of them; Elena didn't feel it biased to call herself Sgt. White's favorite. Even where Oscar was the better soldier, Elena was the better apprentice.

She supposed, in a way, she had helped him turn into the vicious person he was. She fostered, rather than assuaged, their competition, and she hadn't missed an opportunity to lord over him whenever possible.

Now, however, it seemed she would pay for it, given the malicious glint in his eye.

"You sound surprised."

"More disappointed," he said, crossing his arms over his chest.

She rolled her eyes. "I wouldn't give you the satisfaction."

He sauntered closer, utilizing his taller and wider frame to seem imposing.

"Things are different now. I'm going to get named second-in-command, and when I do, you'll be licking my boots."

She looked down at said boots and grinned. "Somehow I doubt that," she said.

His eyes narrowed.

"I don't think there's a chance in hell you'd be made second. Sgt. White knows what you're about. You're a brute," she said.

"And you're a traitor," he growled, all the play falling from his face.

Her lips pursed. "Come again?"

"You're. A. Traitor. Everyone knows it. You'd rather sing Kumbaya with the natives than actually do your job. You haven't got the stomach to be a soldier."

Elena sucked in a breath. "You don't know what you're talking about."

A reptilian smile spread over his face, and he pounced on her hesitation. "It's bad enough we

128

got civilians betraying their own species, but a soldier?" He shook his head. "It's pathetic."

"Get out of my face," she said, pushing him away.

He came back at her immediately, knowing he had figured her out. It wasn't that she was considering betraying anybody. She knew General Hammond was wrong. She knew things needed to change. But would she actually take part?

"I'm watching you," he said. "Every minute of every day I'll be watching. You slip up, and I'll be there. We both know it's just a matter of time."

She walked around the other side of her speeder, but he followed. Her pulse pounded in her ears, her fight-or-flight reflex kicking in. She worried which one would win.

"Yeah? And who's watching you," she countered, satisfied to see him caught off guard. "You're a ticking time bomb. You're undisciplined and crazy if you think anyone would give you a promotion."

He loomed over her, but she stood her ground.

This had been coming for a while now. Best to get it over with.

"If I ever find out you've betrayed us, I'll make you sorry."

She leaned as close as she could without gagging. "I'd like to see you try."

All she did was wait for the slight movement, a step back, and she jammed her head up into his chin.

He grunted, stumbling back, but was ready for her when she came at him again, throwing his hands up.

Elena jabbed at his chest then went for his head when he defended himself. He caught her hand, twisted it in his larger one, nearly broke her arm.

She refused to cry out, instead going with the twisting motion to get her other arm around. She jabbed at his face, went for eyes.

"Hey, hey, hey!"

Oscar stepped back suddenly, almost popping Elena's arm out of socket as he went.

She staggered forward, holding her arm gingerly. When she turned around, she found a scowling Sgt. White in between them.

"I turn my back for a minute and you're already at each other's throats! God in heaven, where did I go wrong with you two?"

Elena almost told her it was Oscar who started it but held in her juvenile excuse. Her chest filled with hot anger at Oscar getting her into trouble with the sergeant.

"What's it this time?" she demanded.

Oscar and Elena glared at one another, neither saying anything until the other would.

The sergeant looked between them, and when she realized neither would be the first to speak, she sighed. "And here I thought you'd grown up. Look, I understand you're both competitive. I think a little competition is healthy, but you two are endangering the whole Vanguard with this feud of yours. Put it behind you."

Finally Elena said, "Yes, ma'am."

Oscar managed a nod.

"Good." She turned to Oscar and said, "Back to work with you. Those crates aren't going to load themselves."

With another stiff nod, and glare at Elena, he headed over to the two cruisers waiting to be loaded with assorted plans, tools, and material. They were bound for San Angelo, to help in their reconstruction.

"What's the matter with you lately?" Sgt. White asked quietly. "You're having trouble getting back into the swing of things."

Elena glanced at Oscar over the sergeant's shoulder and saw she was getting an evil sneer for receiving softer words from Sgt. White.

"Nothing. I'm fine, I just didn't want to deal with him today."

"So instead you wanted to fight him?"

"I didn't say it was a good idea."

Sgt. White grinned wryly. "Good, because you'd be wrong." She looked Elena up and down, a pensive look on her face. Elena was about to ask if something was the matter when she continued, in barely more than a whisper, "Is something going on?"

"What d'you mean?"

Looking about for a moment, Sgt. White motioned for her to follow her to an empty corner of the hangar. Elena could feel Oscar boring a hole in the back of her head with his eyes.

Turning on her, Sgt. White asked, "You'd tell me if you were in trouble, wouldn't you?"

"That'd depend on the type of trouble."

Sgt. White frowned. "Elena, be serious."

Sobering, Elena's eyes fell to the ground. "I'm not in trouble."

When she finally raised her head again, she found the sergeant looking at her thoughtfully. If this was an interrogation, it was an unorthodox one.

"I just want you to be careful," she said, "whatever it is you're doing."

"I'm not—"

Sgt. White put her hand up. She looked around again and took a step closer, to be sure only Elena heard her when she said, "You need to look sharp. Reports have just come in—there's been an enormous influx of population in the native capital. That queen's amassing an army, and we think it'll be here soon."

Elena looked at her, startled. "Should you be telling me this?"

The sergeant's look answered the question for her.

"What should we do?" she asked.

"My orders are to start preparing—drilling starts back up tomorrow and we're going to need to make safe the new colony. What you'll do is entirely up to you."

"What d'you—?"

"Elena, I want you to do what you think is right."

And with a nod, the sergeant left her standing

there, baffled. What in the world did she mean, it was up to her? What sort of orders were those?

Elena stood rooted to the spot, a realization slowly trickling into her mind. Sgt. White thought Elena's allegiance was shifting too. But she hadn't seemed angry about it—what then? What did she think Elena was going to do, relay it to the opposition?

The instant that hit her mind, Elena knew that's exactly what she needed to do. She hoped she was right to think the sergeant wanted her to pass this on, believing she had contacts in the opposition. Well, she would be right.

Her breathing was erratic as she typed up a hasty invitation to Cass to meet for dinner that night. She would tell Cass then and hope that would gain her access to the opposition and to Carter. They would know what to do with the information—a native army could be the downfall or ascendancy of General Hammond. Perhaps the opposition would know how to make the former happen.

She did the rest of her daily tasks with a sort of excited, anxious alacrity, all the while considering how strange it felt to be in opposition.

The courtyard was such an epicenter of noise and activity that Rhys didn't realize Yaro was walking towards him until he was feet away. Grinning up at the stoic warrior, Rhys gestured at the production line the humans had going.

"We work hard," he said.

Yaro nodded. "It is good work. The queen is pleased."

Rhys couldn't help glancing over at Ondra, the younger warrior who oversaw the Charneki's part of the project, as Yaro said this. Most of the time he stood there silently, his mouth downturned in disdain, until he needed to give an order. Rhys had tried multiple times to coax him into conversation, but the proud Charneki wouldn't have it, preferring to reply with scowls. Rhys couldn't quite figure out why Ondra, if he had such a strong distrust of the humans, had been assigned to oversee the generators' construction, but he had guessed already that Ondra was close with the queen. Apparently that was reason enough. Still, it bemused him.

Ondra's mistrustful presence kept Rhys on edge, for it made it harder for him to hide those small sabotage attempts by the five soldiers. They refused to come around, instead acting upon their anger by breaking anything having to do with the generators if someone didn't watch them. It had been small so far, just minor components and parts, but Rhys knew they couldn't afford this getting back to the Charneki. Ondra, then, didn't make running damage control easy.

"We should be done soon," Rhys said. "Have you come to see it?"

"Your new machines are not of this world. Still,

I hope they may help. I have come, however, to take you to the Red Hall. The queen will see you."

"Oh, good!" he said. "That is kind of her. Will we go now?"

"Yes."

Rhys nodded and walked quickly over to tell Cara where he was going.

"All right, then. But don't think I'll do your work for you," she said with a playful smile. "Oh, and tell her we should be ready by the day after tomorrow."

"Will do!" Rhys said over his shoulder, heading back to Yaro.

He was in conference with Ondra, who quieted the instant Rhys came within earshot.

Yaro gave him a look. "Still you doubt her will?"

"I do what is asked of me."

Yaro leaned in closer, but Rhys could still hear him say, "Would it hurt you so much to be polite?"

Ondra's gaze slid over to him, and he replied, "It might."

Yaro grunted and turned on his heels, leaving Rhys to jog to catch up.

"I have not seen you in many days," Rhys said when he walked alongside Yaro.

"There has been much to do." He looked down at Rhys. "But I am happy to see you now, little one."

Rhys grinned, but it didn't quite reach his eyes. The reminder that the Charneki were preparing for war sobered him. He thanked his lucky stars the project would be completed before their leaving for the north, but he was beginning to doubt these generators, or anything they could build, would stop the coming battle. That's why Rhys had asked to see the queen. He had one last thing to offer.

"Ondra does not like me," Rhys said.

"He is young. And sometimes foolish."

"I am young. Am I foolish too?" he asked with a grin.

Yaro gazed down at him and slowly a smile spread across his face. "We shall see!"

"Still," Rhys said as they headed down a colonnaded corridor, "I wish he would like me. Or at least not scowl so much."

"He does not trust you, little *plarra*. You are, after all, a *plarra*."

Rhys was still unsure about the translation of *plarra*, but guessing from similar words, he thought it meant something like 'demon.' It seemed to be used instead of 'human.'

"But the queen—"

"The queen trusts you. Of that you can be sure. But you will have to convince others."

"Will I ever convince him?"

Yaro glanced down at Rhys. "You must be patient with him. He may yet surprise you."

Yaro spoke with fondness, piquing Rhys's interest, but they soon arrived at the entrance to the throne room so that he couldn't ask.

His heart thudded in his chest, and he looked up at Yaro for some reassurance.

The big warrior nodded at him. "She is waiting for you."

Thanking him, Rhys sucked in a long breath before heading into the cool room. Spring was upon them now, the days warming and the second sun, Undin, emerging from behind the larger one, Nahara, which Terra Nova orbited.

He was a little surprised to find it so empty, only three Elders, including the blind one who always sat beside the throne, and the queen herself on the opposite end of the room. He walked towards them, Yaro not far behind.

"Hello, Rhys," said the queen once he was close.

"Greetings, queen," he said, bowing to her. "I am glad to see you."

"I trust nothing is wrong with our project?"

"No, queen, nothing is wrong. In fact, I have been instructed to tell you we should finish within two days, and hope you will come to see."

She nodded. "I am happy to hear this. We will have a night demonstration."

She clapped once. From a side door Rhys hadn't noticed before, a Charneki with a leather strip round its neck, with what looked like a stamped clay medallion hanging from it, walked quickly to the throne.

To this Charneki the queen said, "Have it made known that in two nights we shall be testing the generators. No one is to worry, it is only light that we have made, and all are encouraged to watch the night sky for it."

"Yes, queen," the attendant said, bowing to her. He was gone almost as quickly as he had come.

"I am pleased to be leaving my city with new protection. I believe these will work nicely."

"We are all glad to be useful to you, queen." He chewed on his bottom lip for a moment, trying to pick his words correctly before proceeding. "I do have something to ask of you."

She looked at him, curious. "If it is in my power."

"I wish to be useful to you still, queen. I wish to go north with you."

The queen looked like she had seen a ghost, her eyes widening and all cheer falling from her face. Her nostrils flared a little as she took a breath, and Rhys waited anxiously for her to say something.

"Have I misspoken, queen? I do not mean to—"

She held a hand up, silencing him. "I am sure it is a noble request," she said finally, "but this is not your war to fight."

"Please, queen, I wish to help."

She smiled, though Rhys was confused why the smile seemed sad.

He glanced up at Yaro and found the warrior looked as grave as the queen.

"I would not run," he said. "You must not think that I would betray you."

The queen held her hand up again. "It is not that, Rhys. I . . . the last time this was asked of me, I agreed to it, to my evermore regret." Her eyes were faraway and glassy. "I returned to Karak without my brother."

Rhys's mouth hung open, for he couldn't form a response. The mention of Zaynab made his heart sting.

"I could not bear the guilt if some terrible fate befell you," she said.

"I do not want to fight, queen. I would be a useless warrior. Besides, the humans are my kin. I cannot fight them."

"Then why do you wish to go north?" asked the old Elder sitting beside the queen.

"I believe I can help. If I go north, the humans will see that you have been kind to me, and I can tell them that the others are well too. I can speak both the Charneki and the human language so that both you and the humans may talk to each other."

The queen smiled at this, though it was still sad. "Do you never lose hope?"

Rhys shook his head. "I do not want war."

This seemed to strike her. "Nor do I." Standing, the queen stepped off the dais and gazed down at Rhys. She placed her hand on his head. "I cannot promise your safety, little one, but you will come north with me."

He smiled. "Thank you, queen. I shall make you proud."

8

lena and Cass walked close together through the haziness of dusk. The lamp-posts were on, and light spilled out onto the street from illuminated windows, but they tried to skirt these pools, knowing it was safest to stay in the shadows. If they were caught, Cass would at best be thrown in prison for an indefinite sentence. Elena could only make morbid guesses at what a soldier's punishment would be.

"You're sure about this?" Cass asked.

"Yup."

"Okay, then. Let me see it."

Elena raised her arm and pushed up the sleeve,

letting Cass at her gauntlet. Opening up a command prompt, Cass quickly typed in a series of code, and the screen's color changed from blue to green.

"That should be enough time," she said, exiting out of the projected keyboard.

Elena didn't understand exactly what Cass had done, but there were those in the opposition who were good with code and technology, able to deaden gauntlets for a brief span of time before Headquarters discovered it and rebooted the system, bringing everything back online. This wasn't the first example of Cass's hacking skills that Elena had seen; she had gotten help creating an encrypted transmission so that she could talk, unmonitored, to Elena and Hugh while they journeyed south.

Popping her jacket collar, Elena pressed the cold tip of her nose into the warm cloth. All were anxious for the advent of spring, but nights were still bitterly cold.

Cass looked around a moment before leading

them on. They rounded a corner, heading deep into the residential quadrant. Coming to a three-story apartment building, Cass began hopping up the steps to the third level. Elena followed her down the corridor, stopping before a closed door.

Cass pulled her right hand out of her glove and pressed it against the monitor. It blinked red, and she entered a five-digit code into the command prompt. The door slid open.

The room inside was spacious but poorly lit. Elena could barely make out any of the dozen or so faces standing around in the main room, and she fought her instinctual hesitation to follow Cass in.

"Ah, good, we can start now."

Ulysses Carter emerged from a murky back corner and smiled at them. He looked Elena up and down. "It's about time," he said. "I've been waiting for you to come around for months."

Elena's eyebrows shot up at that, but Carter just laughed, ushering them further inside.

"Sorry about the dark. We find it's better to make it look like no one's home."

"Is everyone here?" asked Cass.

"Yes, ma'am."

There wasn't enough furniture in the living room to accommodate all of them, so Elena stood rigidly next to but slightly behind Cass. Her pulse pounded in her head to think she was actually at a resistance meeting.

It hadn't taken much to convince Cass. She listened to Elena's report and agreed that the opposition should hear it. If there was anyone who could do something with it, it was Carter. The hard part had been waiting to hear back if she would be allowed anywhere near the opposition. Whatever Cass had said worked.

Once her eyes adjusted and Elena was able to look at some of the others gathered, she realized she recognized some. A few she had seen helping Carter officiate the old public forums. She even saw the woman who lived two apartments down.

Most of them wouldn't meet Elena's gaze, and she remembered that having military personnel present couldn't put them at ease.

"All right then," Carter said, his voice somehow louder in the near-dark. "Everyone, I'd like you to meet Elena Ames of the Vanguard Platoon."

The room stayed painfully silent, the others assessing Elena.

She nodded.

Looking at the others himself, Carter said, "I'll admit, I was skeptical when Cass came to me. I've hoped for a while, though, that we'd be able to get more military personnel on our side, Elena in particular—she's been to the native city and can tell us just how much Hammond is lying about them."

"We don't need her to tell us that."

"Maybe not. But Cass has vouched for her, and when have we ever had reason to doubt Cass?"

Just to drive the point home, Cass smiled at

everyone with a disarming sweetness Elena knew all too well.

"Why've you come now?" asked a man across the room.

"She has some information for us," Cass said.

"We're all ears," said Carter.

Elena sucked in a breath, trying to order the words right in her mind. She didn't want to let on how much the others unnerved her. She knew how she must look to them, could see most were wondering if she was a spy.

"I've had information that there's a native army amassing in the capital. Scans show a spike in population density and activity. How soon they'll march isn't known yet, but it has to be soon."

Several eyebrows rose, but Elena didn't have much time to think before she was confronted with, "Who's this information from?"

She looked over at the short-haired woman who had asked. "A reliable source," she said, holding in her cringe. This was going to go over real well.

The woman scoffed. "Oh, this is bull!"

"I think we're going to need a little more," Carter said, crossing his arms.

Elena swallowed the lump in her throat. Her dander was up, suddenly feeling the need to defend Sgt. White. Going to the opposition leaders was her own decision. What the sergeant had meant for her to do with the information she couldn't say for certain, and she didn't want to drag Sgt. White into something she might not want to be involved with.

"It's from a senior military official. I'd rather not reveal her name, if it's all right. She told me in confidence, and if either of us are sniffed out, you don't have an inside source."

The others looked amongst themselves.

"Can you trust her?" a tall, lean man next to Carter asked.

She nodded. "With my life."

Her gaze slid back to Carter, and she watched the cogs of his mind working overtime. He remained silent for several long moments, the group giving way to quiet chatter. When he did speak, he asked something Elena didn't expect: "And what d'you want us to do with this information?"

Her mouth slightly open, she stared at him. A prickly dislike washed over her; she was getting sick of tests.

"Well, this is the war the general wants," Cass said, giving her a small nudge for encouragement.

Elena cleared her throat. "Yeah, it'll play right into her hands. Depending on how it goes, not only can she rally support here, she can convince San Angelo that the threat is real."

"We've been faced with native attacks before and she didn't get much support," said the short-haired woman.

"She's already had a surge in recruitment from the speech she gave not long ago. The military's already doubled its numbers. If she can do that with a speech, just think what an actual threat could do." Elena watched, satisfied, as the argument died in the woman's throat.

"If we know that they're coming, maybe we can make plans, take away any advantage she might gain from it."

"And how would we do that?" Carter asked.

Elena had the feeling he had already figured out what he was going to say and do, but wanted to see what she would say.

"We would need to tell those in San Angelo. Take away the surprise element. If they're warned, they can take their own precautions and be ready instead of relying on us here."

"Good," Carter said with a nod. "I'll pass it along to my contacts there. You're right, they definitely should be warned."

Though she had suggested it, Elena didn't know how he managed to have contacts in San Angelo. No one from New Haven was allowed there anymore unless on official business. It wasn't that the colonies hated each other. Quite the opposite, actually. So many in New Haven liked what was going on in San Angelo—saw what could have been their own colony had someone other than General Hammond been in charge—that there had been waves of people secretly emigrating there. Only a few got in; most were asked to return to New Haven since the new colony had to support its own people first.

Asked to deal with it, General Hammond responded in her usual fashion by implementing an even stricter curfew and setting up border patrol. The perimeter around New Haven was always on now, ready to electrocute anyone, outside or in, who came anywhere close.

"Now, I've a mind to do something, but things will need to happen before we can do it." Carter looked to Elena and Cass. "Do you two think it'd be possible to get our hands on a DL?"

Elena had brought Rhys's Dialect Library, an advanced translation device, back from the Charneki city, complete with everything he knew of their language and what it heard during their time there. With the help of Rhys's DL, they had been able to almost completely translate the Tikshi language, which was an offshoot of Charneki.

While the DL's stored information had been downloaded onto several other devices, namely the gauntlets of those who had gone south, no one could access the program without a code.

She told Carter as much.

"That shouldn't be too much of a problem," he said. "We should be able to work out a hack in time."

"But why?" asked the short-haired woman.

Carter grinned. "It's a risky, near-impossible plan, I know, but by now you shouldn't expect anything less from me. I'm thinking, if we can get an accurate time frame of when the natives should be close, we find a way out of New Haven and approach them."

"And what'll that do?" asked the man standing beside Cass.

"Well, for one thing, it should show them that we're divided. They would think it to their advantage, and we can offer to help them if they help us. If we can negotiate with them, we might be able to use their threat as an advantage. If New Haven and San Angelo see humans peacefully talking with natives, Hammond won't have any ground to stand on."

"The last time we tried to negotiate with them, things didn't go so well, to say the least," the short-haired woman said.

"How do we know they'll listen?" asked another woman.

"The queen has seen me before," Elena found herself saying. "And if she doesn't recognize me, the native we held captive might. He's one of her top warriors. He might listen to us."

Carter clapped his hands together, smiling. "I knew you'd come around. Welcome to the opposition!"

9

Hugh braced himself against the door, clenching his jaw, as Saranov swerved around a wide puddle, no doubt hiding a cavernous pothole. Rain beat down on the windshield, the wiper blades at their wit's end trying to keep it clear, and Saranov laughed, almost manically, in the seat beside him.

"God, I love driving!" he said.

Hugh grimaced.

A hard *thump* came from the back of the vehicle, the six other engineers in the rear no doubt having a worse time of it than Hugh.

In the first vehicle in a caravan of three headed

to San Angelo, Saranov, Hugh, and the others were bound to help put the finishing touches on the new colony's power plant while their military escort picked up spare equipment. Hugh doubted anyone in San Angelo knew the spare parts were going to a weapon of mass destruction; Kimura, who had been elected leader for one term—or two Terra Novan years—didn't seem like the type to condone such a thing, native threat or no.

Hugh gripped the door handle with white knuckles as the cruiser slid a yard off the road. While a good strong rain was a sort of novelty to them—the only rainstorms Hugh could remember on Earth dropped acid rain—it still made for bad driving. He glanced at the projected map screen on the dash and contented himself that there were only five miles to go.

The road was well worn by now with the traffic that went to and from San Angelo, but it was still dirt. New Haven's head civil engineer had decided to hold off on laying concrete until summer.

Bringing it down a gear, the cruiser hummed, wanting to go faster. Saranov kept it slow, navigating the half-washed-away road, and Hugh felt blessed that they were going under twenty.

"Do you think she'll actually use it?" Hugh found himself asking.

Saranov glanced over at him. "Her weapon?"

Hugh nodded.

"Can't say. It depends on what the natives do now."

"You don't think she's just going to drop it once we finish?"

"Why all the questions?"

Hugh began picking at his thumb. "Rhys's in that city," he said. "If she sets if off there, he'll be . . ."

Saranov cleared his throat. "We can't know anything for sure."

"You mean he might already be dead."

"No, that's not . . . " He sighed. "Hugh, you can't think like that."

"Is there something I could do, you think?" The question was more for himself than Saranov, not really realizing he had said it out loud. "She doesn't care about them anymore—she won't try to get them out. D'you think someone else could? Maybe get a message through? D'you think . . . maybe the opposition could help?"

His words hung in the cab for an uncomfortable moment. Hugh realized what he was saying and turned red. Saranov was no friend of General Hammond, but he wasn't sure sometimes just how much his former mentor disagreed with what went on. If he did whole-heartedly, he never showed it.

"Hugh, I know you're worried about him. I understand. You'll see him again—I have a feeling. You'll get him back somehow. But for now I think you need to bide your time. There's a lot at stake, and one misstep could ruin it. You need to be sure. For now, stay the course."

Saranov's speech was all at once comforting and disappointing. Hugh had actually worked himself into a sort of excited fervor, his mind whirring with ideas of how to get Rhys out, who to talk to, if he even dared think about joining the opposition. Saranov's advice snapped him back into reality. He knew he lost himself for a moment there, and knew that he couldn't get carried away. Saranov was right—a lot was at stake. He couldn't afford a mistake now, not with Rhys's life possibly hanging in the balance.

Hugh nodded once. "Yeah, you're probably right."

He could feel Saranov glancing at him, but he kept his eyes on the road. The rest of the trip was silent.

When they arrived at San Angelo's northeastern gate, they waited a moment for the perimeter section to deactivate before driving through. Saranov steered them into the heart of the industrial quadrant where the power plants stood.

After the cruiser came to a stop, Hugh threw his hood over his head and slid out of the vehicle, hitting sopping wet ground. His mood darkened instantly. He didn't like being wet, acid rain or no.

The other engineers hopped out of the back of the cruiser as Saranov and Hugh waved at the waiting Keaton standing in the doorway of the power plant.

They turned at the sound of Saranov's name being called.

The two other cruisers eased up next to them, and the passenger window of the first rolled down.

"Keep this quick," said Colonel Klein with a stern look. "We need to get back as soon as possible."

"Why?" Saranov asked.

"Native hostiles have been spotted in the surrounding area. The sooner we're done here, the sooner we can get back and you can finish the package."

"Ah, yes. Wouldn't want to be late."

The colonel and Saranov glared at each other

for an uncomfortable moment before Klein finally nodded stiffly, barked a command to his driver, and drove on.

Saranov and Klein had been friends once, but not since Hugh made a dash for the native capital to warn Rhys and the others that their mission was a trap. Klein had almost shot Hugh. Saranov stopped him.

Turning around, Saranov caught Hugh's gaze. He clapped his back, sending little droplets off his raincoat.

The team trudged into the power plant, shaking out sopping hair and coats before following Keaton into the bowels of the plant.

Hugh shook his hand as they walked.

"You've been a stranger," Keaton said with a smile. "Lots to do at home?"

Hugh cleared his throat. "Something like that."

"Well, we're happy to have all you here now. Everyone's excited to get this show on the road."

"Wouldn't miss it."

"There're a lot of people ready for electricity, let me tell you."

"Ha, I'll bet. I can't tell you how miserable it is here in winter without a heating unit."

Keaton made a playfully horrified face, and the two of them laughed.

The San Angelo starships numbering almost double those of New Haven meant almost double the engines. The central engine room stood like a huge warehouse of manufactured power, each of the former starship engines lined up, main engine and six auxiliary, in seven rows with thirty yards between each row.

They walked to the first main engine which had belonged to their flagship, and from there the New Haven engineers split up with San Angelo's to go work on the other six rows.

Goggles were passed around before they got to work, and with the extra hands from New Haven, it was quick work putting the finishing touches on the generators. When confirmation came that all rows were ready, Keaton smiled.

"Here we go!"

He typed in the command, his finger hovering over the "ENTER" button.

An alarm sounded, red lights flashing across the ceiling.

Saranov, Hugh, and Keaton looked at each other, bemused.

"Is it the generators?" Hugh asked.

Keaton's fingers flew across the project keyboard, running diagnostics again, and he shook his head. "No, everything says—"

"It's the perimeter alarm," Saranov said.

Hugh and Keaton turned to him. He was looking down at a projected video feed on his gauntlet.

A monotone voice announced in the background what they could see plain as day on Saranov's gauntlet: A native army crested the hills due west. The rain had stopped, and their colorful skin and the shells of their beasts glistened in the tenuous daylight. Soaked banners stood starkly against the cloudy sky behind them, a rainbow of colors advertising thousands of natives.

"I thought they weren't coming here . . . ?" Hugh heard Keaton mutter.

He didn't have time to think about it. He grasped Saranov's wrist, leaning in closer to the screen. Was he seeing things? In the front lines—was that . . . ?

———————

The alarm echoed through the hangar, jarring Elena's brain against her skull. Waking from her momentary daze, her training kicked in. She was one of the first to her locker, extracting body suit, pack, ammo belt.

"*Native hostiles spotted, native hostiles spotted,*" reported the female monotone voice over their gauntlet speakers.

"Any useful information?" Elena asked under her breath as Sgt. White zipped up her suit.

"It's everybody."

Elena's brows shot up at that. Everybody? All the platoons? How many natives, exactly?

Elena followed behind the sergeant, who barked orders for cruisers and speeders. She reached out a hand and stopped Elena from making it to her speeder.

"What's the—?"

"Not you," she said quietly.

"What? Why?"

"You're sticking with me."

Elena made a face.

"I'm supposed to monitor you directly," she said. "General's orders."

Sgt. White kept the rest of her face expressionless, but Elena could see in her eyes that the order didn't sit well with her. Well, that made two of them.

The hangar became an orchestrated cacophony of preparation, engines humming to life, guns mounting, soldiers lining up in formation. In a matter of minutes the whole Vanguard Platoon stood at attention just outside the hangar door.

A light mist dampened their battle suits as the other platoons emerged from their respective hangars. All six platoons, three-thousand soldiers, stood there in the mud.

General Hammond didn't keep them waiting long. From the direction of Headquarters came a blockade of ten armored cruisers, and the lead one stopped just in front of Vanguard's hangar. From the passenger seat, the general appeared, holding herself up between the door and roof of her cruiser.

"This is the moment we've feared," she said in her best boom. "A native army is approaching San Angelo as we speak. We've been preparing for this day, and now that it's come, let's go show those natives who deserves to be the master of this world! Stations! We head out in two minutes!"

Soldiers streamed into the cruisers and mounted speeders, all ready with time to spare for the countdown.

Hopping up into the passenger seat, Elena's door slammed shut just as Sgt. White stepped on the gas, following close behind the general's block-ade.

They had barely made it outside the New Haven perimeter when Sgt. White's gauntlet flashed. Accepting the incoming message, General Hammond's face stared back at the sergeant.

"I want this nice and clean, White," she said. "A real show for San Angelo."

"Ma'am, I thought they were headed for us, not them?"

Elena thought the general did a bad job of hiding her obviously pleased grin.

"Apparently not. But that doesn't matter. We'll show San Angelo and Kimura just how much they need us. Nice and clean."

"Yes, ma'am."

The general nodded and then was gone.

Elena thought she should be surprised but wasn't. Of course the general would play this to her advantage. Elena doubted the general ever thought the native army was coming for New Haven. How perfect it was. The new colony, unprepared for war—General Hammond comes in the hero, laying to rest any more hesitation in San Angelo. Her resources, men, and material, would double, maybe even triple.

"So how're we gonna play this?" Elena asked.

"We're going to follow orders." Sgt. White sounded like she had something lodged in her throat.

Elena glanced at her from the corner of her eye. She couldn't face her when she asked, her voice barely more than a whisper, "You don't think it's wrong?"

"We have to defend ourselves."

"Well, yeah, but . . . "

Sgt. White reached over and put a hand on Elena's shoulder. "My top priority is making sure you get through this."

"What d'you—?"

"You know you're under scrutiny. You can't mess up, not now."

"But I . . . "

"Elena, listen to me." Elena couldn't help looking over, her gaze drawn by the sergeant's tone. "You have such a good heart. I know you don't always see it, but I do. You're going to change this world."

Elena let out a breath in a half-hearted scoff. "By slaughtering natives?"

Sgt. White looked at her for a long moment. "You're going to live to fight another day."

"What're you talking about?"

"You're right—this's wrong. This whole thing. But right now, it's what we have to do to keep you alive. Don't you understand? This's a test. The general wants to see your loyalty. And you're going to prove it today."

Elena rubbed her temple. "I'm tired of killing."

"I know. But today it's them or you. And I'll be damned if it's you. I won't let her do anything to you, but for now I need you to do what I say. We get through this. You do as you're ordered."

Elena sighed but couldn't help looking at Sgt. White again. She couldn't refuse, not when it was the sergeant, her mother, asking.

"Fight another day?" she said, forcing herself to swallow her disgust.

The sergeant nodded. "Another day. Soon."

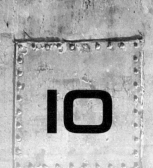

10

"Hugh, wait!"

Hugh skidded to a stop as Saranov tugged him back by the collar of his jacket. Mud and droplets went spraying everywhere as the two men stood on the top of a small berm, looking out at the low hills to the west. Behind them stood San Angelo's industrial quadrant, and not far off, they could hear yelling from the military quadrant. Full mobilization had been ordered at the sight of the coming native army, now just under a mile away.

"I saw him; I know I did!"

"What would Rhys be doing with the native army?"

He knew Saranov spoke sense, but his heart pounded in his ears, the fleeting image of Rhys among the ranks of natives burned into his mind.

Saranov opened his mouth to say something, but his gaze was caught by something else. He turned his head. "What in the world are they doing?"

Hugh tore his eyes from the native front line, which had come to a stop, to follow Saranov's gaze. His brows shot up when he saw a group of about a dozen humans arguing with a perimeter guard. The guard nodded and begrudgingly pressed a series of commands on his gauntlet. The perimeter flashed light blue and then was gone.

"Are they—?"

"That's Montgomery with them."

"Who?" Hugh asked.

"One of Kimura's aides."

"What's he doing? Is Kimura letting them talk with the natives?"

That seemed exactly what was going to happen. The dozen humans marched from the perimeter, down the hill, and started across the small, grassy valley between hills.

"Wait, isn't that Keaton?" Hugh couldn't believe the words that came from his mouth. He looked around, as if expecting to find Keaton among the other engineers who had come up behind him and Saranov.

Saranov fished in his pocket before pulling out a pair of specs. He pressed them against his face.

"Yup. What do they think they're doing?"

To their left they heard an increase in noise from the military quadrant. Saranov swung that way with his specs, and Hugh waited anxiously to hear what he could see. If he squinted, Hugh could make out cruisers and speeders emerging from hangars.

"Kimura's in one of the lead ones," Saranov said. "He's talking. Now he's saying something into his gauntlet. What's he waiting for?"

Hugh looked back at the human party, and his stomach hit the ground when he saw a dispatch of natives coming out to meet them. It looked to be about six natives atop those lumbering turtle-like creatures they had. The two in the back carried long spears with banners flapping just beneath the blades. The next two wore glimmering golden breastplates with purple feathers adorning the crest of their helmets. And finally in the center was what had to be the queen—dressed in billowing crimson robes and breastplate, her neck and arms were covered in circular plates that resembled necklaces and bracelets, though they moved as she did and seemed to be functional armor. Riding slightly behind her, between her and the bigger of the two helmeted warriors, was a very little native.

No. Not a native.

"Gimme the specs," Hugh said, snatching them up without waiting for Saranov's answer.

He refocused them before zooming in on the approaching native party. He fixed on the little figure and knew immediately it was his brother.

All the breath escaped his lungs, and his pulse was deafening in his ears.

"There he is." He lowered the specs when he felt Saranov's hand on his shoulder. He looked over at him and smiled. "He's alive!"

Hugh's relief threatened to overwhelm him, and he tried to stay focused. Rhys was alive. But he stood where a battle was about to take place. He retrained the specs, his palms growing sweaty. Rhys was saying something to the queen.

"I have to get him outta there," Hugh said. "He'll be a sitting duck if—"

"Wait, wait," Saranov said, keeping him in place, not letting him start down the side of the berm.

Hugh glared at him but found Saranov's eyes on the military quadrant. Without a word Saranov took back the specs and pointed them at Kimura.

From what he could see, the San Angelo forces were amassing in a small plain just in front of the military quadrant, but they weren't moving.

"He's waiting for them," Saranov said.

Hugh motioned for the specs back and got them. He refocused them just in time to see the two groups meet, separated by a small creek running through the valley. Wishing he could hear what they said, he watched as Rhys acted as an intermediary for the natives and humans. He nodded several times, even smiled.

Almost angry at how calm Rhys seemed, Hugh was anxious to do something. Were they negotiating terms? Could Rhys and the humans actually talk the natives out of this? If the natives had come to New Haven, the damp afternoon would already be echoing with gunshots. Was that why they came here instead?

Hugh looked over the dozen humans, and though their backs were to him, he picked Keaton out of the line. They all seemed as relaxed as they could be, and Hugh realized with a shock that none of them were armed.

He trained back on Rhys when he saw his

mouth moving. He nodded. Talked to the queen. Turned back to the humans. Translated.

"Kimura still hasn't moved," Saranov said.

"What're they doing?"

"It looks like they're negotiating, if you can believe it."

"Could that work?"

Saranov let out a breath. "It certainly isn't what Hammond wants."

Hugh's heart lurched into his throat as he watched Rhys and the others jerk their heads to the north. The sound hit Hugh and Saranov a moment later, the sound of gunshots. He turned the specs to his right and saw, cresting a northern rise of hills, what had to be the whole New Haven contingent barreling down upon the natives.

Cannons blasted the ground, flinging dirt everywhere, and the shots came closer and closer to the group in the small valley. The native line erupted into activity, backing out of range. The two parties in the valley scattered, though the cannon blasts seemed to turn away from them when those firing realized humans were down there.

Hugh felt sick to his stomach when he realized he had lost Rhys. He searched frantically for him with the specs, finally found him flanked by the two warriors wearing golden breastplates. He was right behind the queen, heading back to the native line. The army was headed for its queen.

His arms fell to his sides, suddenly feeling cold. He had to do something. But the itch had left him, uncertain now what exactly he had to do.

He surrendered the specs to Saranov, who looked quickly over at Kimura.

"He's arguing with someone—Hammond no doubt. Damn, what a mess."

"My brother's out there."

Saranov turned to look at him. Hugh lifted his gaze to meet Saranov's, and the older man nodded.

"You wanna go get him?"

Hugh swallowed the lump in his throat. "Yeah."

Clapping Hugh's shoulder, Saranov turned

towards the other engineers. "Get back to the power plant. Guard the engines. All hell's gonna break loose."

Ignoring the others' demands to know where they thought they were going, Hugh and Saranov ran for the military quadrant. As they went, they saw Kimura and his troops beginning to file from San Angelo towards the battle. Whatever Hammond had said worked. Though Hugh didn't know how Kimura could refuse with the battle on his doorstep.

They made it to one of the first hangars with several others in civilian dress. They weren't the only ones with the idea. An officer was there taking names and handing out standard plasma rifles. They were decent weapons, but the different humidity of Terra Nova often made them unreliable. Glancing up the sky, Hugh knew it would be a miracle if most of the guns didn't jam. He didn't worry about it too much—the gun was his ticket in.

By the look of it, the native army numbered in the tens of thousands. Hugh was grateful that the humans needed all the extra hands they could get, minimal questions asked. Though, he tried not to think about how they were heading into a battle—his stomach, feeling as if it was collapsing in on itself, threatened to keep him out of the fray.

Hugh and Saranov gave their names and serials quickly, then had to argue for a moment with the officer about why New Haven engineers were here and wanted to fight.

"There's a goddamn army out there, son!" Saranov barked. "Do you really wanna be choosy? We're good shots, and I'll be damned if I'll have my home taken from me."

Which line Saranov fed the young lieutenant was the one that got them the rifles Hugh wasn't sure and didn't care.

His pulse hammering in his head, he wrapped his hands around the rifle. He had promised himself multiple times he would never hold one again, would never kill anything again. But this was different. His brother, his only flesh and blood, the better part of himself, was out there. He needed to get him back.

He nodded at Saranov, and they headed out with a thin line of civilian soldiers to meet the native army.

Her breath coming in short bursts, Zeneba's whole body tingled with vitality as she watched her brave Charneki warriors charge towards her. The lines split around them, engulfing her, Ondra, Yaro, Rhys, and the two banner-bearers.

Once she had been encircled, her army formed as quickly as they could in a defensive circle, the shield-bearers in the front lines. They stood six deep, a hand on the shoulder of the warrior in front, ready to pull themselves forward and their comrade back when it was their turn at the front.

Those shield-bearers around her raised their arms until she and her party stood in a canopy of shields.

"What shall we do, Golden One?"

Zeneba looked over her shoulder to see Chieftain Heta and her *garan*—of the southern type, with a thinner shell but stouter legs that could run faster than their northern cousins—being let through the shields.

"This changes nothing. We have two fronts and more enemies, but today is our day. Yaro," she said, "go with Heta, take Chieftain Samuka, and meet their northern forces. I shall stay with the main army and push forward to their city as we planned."

"It will be done!" Yaro said.

Chieftain Heta nodded and placed her helmet, black as night, on her head. The helmet shimmered like a nightmare in the waning sunlight, which was just poking through the heavy clouds. "I shall show them why they call me Hammer Fist!" she said before ducking under shields.

Yaro made to follow her but paused when his *garan* stood beside Zeneba's.

She reached out her hand and they clasped wrists.

"Nahara bless you," she said.

"And Undin keep you," he replied.

She watched him go. Blinking back tears, she resolved to keep her mind focused. The rhythmic *boom* of the human weapons brought her back, made her attention snap in place.

Turning towards the human city, she saw their forces were advancing, though they had yet to shoot.

"I am sorry, *mara.*"

Looking down at Rhys, who sat on a smaller *garan* and wore a cuirass that had to be adjusted by a smith on their way here, she grinned.

"What have you to be sorry for, little *plarra*? You were glorious."

Rhys's sad expression didn't change. "I think we might have talked more if the others had not come."

"We can sit here all day and speak of ifs, little one, but now I have a battle to manage."

He nodded, his eyes sinking down, so she thought to add, "I am sorry it has come to this too. It was a fool's hope that we might have spoken instead of fought, but I was a fool. The day will come for words, and I hope to have you beside me when it is here. But for now, I must fight for my people. I thank you for your help."

Rhys bowed his head to her and seemed to focus, his eyes sharpening, as he looked out at the coming wave.

Zeneba reached over and took her helmet from Ondra, and placed it on her head. It was a perfect fit, the soft leather interior snug around the scalloped ridges of her headdress. Adjusting herself in the saddle, she gave the command for bow-bearers to take their positions. Arrowheads glinted as they rose towards the gray sky. She nodded, and cries rang out from the Callers to let fly arrows.

Bowstrings sang a unison song as arrows were

loosed upon the afternoon. Zeneba found herself glancing over at Rhys and saw his eyes were closed tight. Turning forward again, her eyes closed too until she heard a harmonious *thunk*.

When she opened them, she saw a sea of lodged arrows covering the valley floor, and several human bodies pinned to the earth. The line of machines had stopped; some had pierced windows, others arrows sticking out of the roof and front. A few jerked to life, pressed against the arrows, and Zeneba watched with small delight as they struggled to break past the wall of tall, thick shafts embedded deep in the ground.

She gave the order for more as a few machines began breaking through, and another volley thickened the arrow wall. When the last arrow lodged, Zeneba held her breath.

Several of the lead machines backed up from the wall, and for a moment she had the fleeting hope this would be the end. Their great weapons lowered, training on the arrow wall, and began firing, great blue blasts sending dirt and arrow shafts everywhere.

Realizing they made to blast their way through, Zeneba gave the order for a third volley.

The bow-bearers had just raised their arrows when screams came from her left flank, and Zeneba turned in time to see those machines that weren't working on the arrow wall now fired at them. The Charneki were in range.

The army began to back up, out of range, and she realized that they would be pushed until they backed up into Yaro and Chieftain Heta.

"Stand fast!" she cried.

The call went down through the ranks, and to the credit of her brave warriors, they held their ground when their *mara* commanded it. But she couldn't stay there, not when her left flank and front line were being hammered steadily away. Sucking in a breath, she knew it was time.

She reached out, and Ondra took up her hand. They glanced at each other and tried to smile.

"Until the end," he said so that only she could hear.

They squeezed the other's hand, then let go.

She gave the order again, and those bow-bearers who could let loose a staggered volley, trying to slow the human advance. All others readied to march.

If Rhys's *garan* hadn't shifted, she would have forgotten he still sat beside her. Her heart thumping, Zeneba realized too late that she should have sent Rhys away, to the back of the army. But there wasn't time. Zeneba could hear more distant gunshots and the sound of heavy fighting to her left and knew sending Rhys to the back of her army would mean putting him in the middle of Yaro and Chieftain Heta's forces.

A stab of regret filled her stomach. How could she let him be here, when it was so dangerous? No, she couldn't send him away—if she did she might never see him again. Best to keep her eye on him, if she could. He was her responsibility now, this brave little human.

"Rhys," she said, drawing his gaze, "I have one last task for you."

"Anything, *mara*."

"You will live today. Do what you must—go to your humans if you have to. I will miss you, but I will rejoice that you are safe. Do this for me?"

He didn't seem to like this command, and she saw the argument rising in his throat, but he managed to stifle it. Instead he nodded. "If you wish."

"I wish for you to live. Ondra—" she looked over at him for a moment "—Ondra will see to you. He will keep you safe."

She breathed a sigh of relief when Ondra nodded, agreeing without protest.

"Stay close to me, *plarra*," he said.

Rhys nodded too.

Zeneba looked out at the incoming humans. They would be here soon. Any moment. Her shield-bearers were once again in the front, eight deep now, ready for them.

She glanced back at Rhys and tried to smile at

him. Putting her hand on his shoulder, she said, "Nahara bless you and Undin keep you, little one. I shall see you when all is done."

"Farewell, *mara*."

Her *garan* began moving down the crest of the hill as drums beat from the back lines, the army marching in time to the imposing beat. Zeneba's heart swelled each time she heard a scream, a cry of pain when a human weapon found its mark, but her Brave Ones earned their name, and marched on to meet the machines.

Having cleared away the arrow wall, human machines and soldiers streamed forwards from the city. As they did, they sent volleys at the Charneki line, but this would not stop Zeneba. Her army got a small reprieve when some human weapons seemed to die, their thunder less deafening. Some soldiers stopped to fix them, leaving a smaller number to charge the Charneki.

The two forces met with a clash of metal, warriors falling upon the human machines, trying to break off the weapons and doors, and pull out the soldiers that were inside. Charneki brought spear and sword down upon the humans, their battle lines remaining strong and true, crashing like a wave upon the human forces. Arrows and spears streaked across the sky, and soon Zeneba found herself towards the front of the battle.

She held her breath. She prayed, asking Nahara and her ancestors to guide her. Then she was at war.

Shield-bearers from her Guard stayed close at all times, but the *mara* herself took human life, setting her spear on a human soldier trying to gun down two of her warriors. She pushed forward with her contingent, and she realized with a triumphant beat of her heart that all of her army pushed forward too. Much more evenly matched up close, the Charneki advanced on the human city.

And that had been her plan along, to threaten the human city, to subdue it, without having to commit too many to death. She warned her chieftans to keep civilian casualties to a minimum. Rhys had convinced her that the humans had nowhere to go—she would allow them to stay, then, but on her terms. This started with the capitulation of the human city.

Shield, spear, sword moved in rhythm, hacking, pushing their way forwards. The human line broke in places. She could see some fleeing back towards the city. Everywhere soldiers were distracted by their noncomplying weapons.

An explosion louder than imagination ricocheted through the valley, drawing everyone's attention to the north. Zeneba's chest panged as she watched, back on the crest of the hill, Yaro and Chieftain Heta's warriors being forced back, freeing some human machines to make towards Zeneba's forces.

She cried out, tried to warn her left flank. Those who heard passed on her command, and a few shield-bearers swung into place before the machines came down on them. Human weapons sprayed shots into them, and Zeneba watched her left flank disintegrate.

Glancing over her shoulder, she knew quickly that she couldn't expect reinforcements from Yaro or Chieftain Heta. Their forces were being backed down the other side of the hill.

Her army was being cut in two, unable to support the other half. She tried to swallow but her throat wouldn't work. Looking up, the human city stood tantalizingly close. She couldn't turn back now, not when she had brought her warriors so far, had preached victory. There had to be some way to turn this around, regroup even—

An impact like a punch to her abdomen sent all the air in her lungs out in one painful gasp. Her hands trembled as she looked down. Blue blood oozed from her open wound, the skin around it feeling on fire. She let out a cry, the pain washing over, throbbing.

Her vision left her for a moment, but she fought to stay conscious. She had to regroup. Clapping an arm over her abdomen, she turned in the saddle to see if anything could be done.

A call around her went out, "Protect the *mara*!" but her warriors couldn't stop the human machines from careening towards them. They hit Charneki bodies, breaking them, as if they were nothing. And they drove straight towards her.

As her warriors grouped around her, she struggled to stay awake. She could feel blood pooling in her lap, running down her leg. She had to fight it. Gripping the hilt of her sword, she faced down the incoming humans.

———

Rhys turned to follow Ondra's gaze, hearing a cry go out. He didn't quite catch what they were saying, but from Ondra's face, it wasn't good. Rhys's gut clenched when he saw the queen keeling over in pain, her hand clutching her left side.

"Zeneba!" Ondra cried, turning his *garan* towards the group amassing around the queen.

He momentarily glanced at Rhys, who nodded, taking his *garan*'s reins in his hands. Ondra spurred his beast onwards, and Rhys, without thinking, followed him.

Adrenaline surged in his head when he saw armored cruisers making for the queen. He glimpsed the sun symbol, the old logo of Dawning Enterprises, on the side of the lead cruiser and knew instantly it was General Hammond. He urged his *garan* on—he needed to get to the queen. He didn't know what he could do, but perhaps, if the general intended to take the queen, he could be taken with her. He would protect her.

He cried out when he felt a hand wrap around his forearm and just caught sight of Ondra's head turning over his shoulder before he fell from his mount.

Struggling against the hands that held him, it

was a moment before he realized the person was saying his name.

His eyes snapped up. "Hugh?"

"Rhys!" Hugh put his hands on either side of Rhys's face. "Thank god! I thought—"

"You have to stop them!"

Hugh glanced over at the swelling battle for the queen. He shook his head.

"We need to get back! *Now!*" Saranov barked, coming up behind Hugh, his gun making a melodious *rat-ta-tat*. Nodding, Hugh gripped Rhys's upper arm and started pulling him towards the city.

"Wait—no—Hugh—we have to—!"

But Hugh wouldn't listen, and Rhys struggled, his neck craning to see what was happening to the queen. His heart sunk to see several cruisers making a wall, one with its back hatch open.

"Watch out!" Saranov called.

They turned to see a warrior bearing down on them. Without thinking, Rhys threw himself in front of their rifles and Ondra.

"*No!*"

Hugh and Saranov looked at him like he was crazy, and he could feel Ondra breathing heavily behind him.

Turning to Ondra, he said quickly, "This is my brother."

Ondra looked between Rhys and Hugh and must have seen the resemblance. He nodded.

"Please, you must help the queen! She needs you. Do not worry about me."

Ondra paused only long enough to extract a dagger and hand it to Rhys. "Stay alive, *plarra*." And then he was off towards the mass still fighting over the queen.

Rhys watched him go, praying he could help save the queen from Hammond. He found himself taking a step forward. Even in the chaos around him, he still wanted to help her.

Hugh's hand landed on his shoulder, and he whirled him around. "We have to get out of here!"

Rhys tried to step back. "I need to help her! Hammond can't get the queen!"

"No, Rhys, we have to get to San Angelo! You'll be safe there."

"Hugh, listen to me, dammit! I'm going to help the queen."

"I'm here to save you."

"I didn't ask you to come!"

"Rhys, wait—!"

"*Incoming!*"

Rhys just barely had time to jump out of the way of a few stray arrows. They lodged in the ground a few feet from him, and for a moment all he could do was sit there, shivering. He had been able to steel his mind up until now, but the reality of the battle around him started to overwhelm him.

He stood up shakily, his balance feeling off. His stomach wasn't doing too well, but he willed it to keep calm.

Movement drew his gaze, and he froze in place, watching Hugh crouch over Saranov. Two arrows stuck out of Saranov's chest, his shirt already bloodying. Rhys saw him blink a few times, knew he was just barely still alive.

Hugh pulled his head up, cradled it, said Saranov's name. A tear ran down his right cheek, making a streak of clean skin on an otherwise dirtied face. Taking a ragged breath, Hugh jumped up, grabbed Saranov underneath the arms, and began dragging him.

It looked difficult; Saranov was the same size as Hugh and probably heavier, and his brother's face strained with effort. The tendons in his neck bulged, sweat and tears running down his face.

"Rhys! Rhys, help me!"

Rhys stood there. He looked at his brother, at the desperation in his eyes. Hugh held in his arms what Rhys knew he considered his father. He was asking for his help.

But that meant giving up the queen. He turned his head, found a clear path to the mass still battling. He couldn't see the queen anymore, but the warriors weren't giving up. That had to be a good sign. Maybe he could still do something.

"Rhys, *please!*"

He felt torn, and he stood like an idiot in the middle of a battlefield thinking about what to do rather than doing anything at all. He hated the inaction, hated himself for having to stop and think about it.

Dashing for Hugh and Saranov, he gripped the older man underneath his right arm and started heaving.

They had made it about twenty yards when Hugh cried, "Rhys, watch out!"

Rhys didn't see anything, just felt Hugh's hands shoving him to the ground. He spluttered, the wind knocked out of him, and heard a few arrows *thunk* into the earth around him.

He heard Hugh groan, and his head shot up. Sticking out of his brother's back was an arrow. Rhys paled.

"It's fine," Hugh said. "Just pull it out."

"W-what?"

"Pull it out. C'mon, we gotta go."

He moved on his hands and knees over to Hugh, watching out for any more stray arrows. About a hundred yards away someone went down, struck. His pulse quickened, and he looked back at his brother.

He wished he hadn't. He wasn't prepared for that old protectiveness that overtook him. He hadn't felt it in such a long time. It should have been him—he should have protected Hugh. That was his job, after all. He took care of them.

With a shaking hand he gripped the shaft of the arrow and with the other steadied himself against Hugh's unhurt left shoulder.

"Ready?"

"Yeah, just do it."

He yanked and fell back from the momentum, the arrow coming with him.

Hugh yelped in pain, his whole body grimacing. Rhys jumped up when he saw Hugh trying to stand. He caught him before he fell onto Saranov. Easing him back down, Rhys said, "No, you stay there."

"We have to get back," Hugh argued.

"You can't even stand, let alone carry someone."

To Rhys's amazement, Hugh chuckled. "This isn't my first arrow. I'll be fine. C'mon, we gotta go."

He managed to stand this time, but when he bent down to pick up Saranov, he almost fell again, wincing in pain.

"Just stay here—I'll find help."

"No, I have to get you to San Angelo, I—"

"Just let me help you, okay? Stay here."

Rhys made to move off, but Hugh said, "Are you going back to them?"

Swallowing hard, Rhys would be lying if he said the thought hadn't crossed his mind. "Of course not," he said, turning back towards Hugh. "I'm not leaving you here."

He reached out and helped Hugh lie down on his side. His brother frowned up at him.

"Yeah?"

"Yeah. I'll be right back with help. Don't move."

"Rhys."

"Hugh, I gotta—"

"It's good to see you."

His eyebrows shot up at that. "Y-yeah," he said. "You too. I'm gonna get help."

Hugh finally let him go, and Rhys retreated from him almost gratefully. Trudging further up the hill, he called out to the first people he came across. The soldiers came running to him when he told them there were wounded, and he led them to Hugh and Saranov.

As two soldiers lifted up Saranov and another supported Hugh, Rhys looked back down at the valley. The Charneki army had been reduced to isolated pockets, the line broken. They were being pushed across the valley, some even back up the slope.

It was done. The cruisers were driving away, leaving behind a pile of Charneki and human bodies. He couldn't tell anything more than that. He was too tired to consider what had happened.

Rhys jogged to catch up with the soldiers and Hugh. He put his brother's arm over his shoulder and bore some of his weight.

Hugh looked down at him.

"Thanks," Rhys said. And he meant it. That was probably the dumbest, bravest thing he had ever seen Hugh do. What had he been thinking?